To MA

"This well-written romance thriller puts me on a roller coaster ride."

Marelene
@melovebook

THE PUBLISHER

SIMPSON MUNRO

This paperback edition published 2021 by Jasami Publishing Ltd
an imprint of Jasami Publishing Ltd
Glasgow, Scotland
https://jasamipublishingltd.com

ISBN 978-1-913798-32-1

Copyright © Simpson Munro 2021

Visit JasamiPublishingLtd.com to read more about all our books and to purchase them. You will also find features, author information and news of any events, also be the first to hear about our new releases.

Acknowledgements

May Winton
Grace Harley
Sigrid Persson

My Editors
May Winton
Grace Harley

First, I wish to sincerely thank May Winton for once again reviewing my work. Through her patience, knowledge, and understanding of language I am learning how important the editing process is, and the perseverance that is required. She is a constant inspiration to me to continue to improve my writing.

Grace brought yet another female perspective to Yvonne's character. Grace, you should be very proud of your input into this book and I thank you. I wish you so much good fortune in your future life.

Jasami's Marketing Team is stellar, and I would like to personally thank Sigrid Persson for all her hard work and creativity in marketing my work.

Finally, I want to thank my publisher, Jasami Publishing Ltd. Michèle believed in this book from the very beginning and has supported me through this process.

May, Grace, Sigrid and Michèle my heartfelt thanks.

Dedication

This book is dedicated to my children and my children's children.

Table of Contents

Simpson Munro

Prologue

At five o'clock precisely, Yvonne Duncan rose from her desk and shut down her computer. If there was one thing that she was particular about, it was starting and finishing her day in the office on time – gone were the days of burning the midnight oil for her.

She made her way to Charing Cross railway station, only one stop east of Partick. As she stood on the platform, she indulged in her favourite pastime, people watching until her train emerged from the long, dark tunnel that connected to Queen Street station. She stood next to the automatic doors throughout the four-to-five-minute journey. She left the Partick platform, and came out at the bus station, which was bustling with commuters waiting for the buses that would take them home. It was at times like these she was grateful for her nearby top-floor tenement flat since it meant she did not have to wait in those long queues.

Walking out onto Dumbarton Road, known for its bustling shops and pubs, she stopped at her local store to pick up a few groceries. Browsing the shelves, she spotted a man mimicking her movements one aisle over. In his mid-to-late twenties, he stood slightly over six feet tall, with long jet-black hair brushed back into a ponytail. A moustache and goatee, both as dark as his hair, was waxed and twisted into a tight spiral. He dressed like a rock star, with a white V-neck vest, black leather trousers that fit snugly against his body under the long black leather coat, and the heavyset pair of goth-style boots added to his height. Four chunky silver rings adorned his right hand like a knuckle duster while a black glove on his left hand completed the ensemble. His piercing steely blue eyes, like those of an eagle searching for its prey, glanced in her direction. As he opened the door to leave the shop, he turned his head and caught her looking over at him. He nodded and smiled, while she quickly handed her milk and bread to the shopkeeper, Asraf, whom she had known for years.

Once she paid for the items, she left the shop quickly with the hope of catching sight of the mysterious stranger again. She spotted him as he turned into a close directly opposite her own. She crossed the busy road, dodging slow-moving cars that were packed nose-to-tail in the evening rush hour, eager to get home.

Yvonne pushed open the security door and began climbing the grey stone stairs worn by almost one hundred years of use. The ornate black iron balusters were fixed to the original mahogany handrail finished with highly polished small brass knobs maintained by the occupants who took pride in their close. Reaching the top floor, she took her keys from her pocket, unlocked the door, and once she locked the door tightly behind her, she began her routine; laying her briefcase on the floor in the hallway, placing her shoes neatly beside the briefcase, checking her flat room by room, and once this was done, she knew she was alone and safe in her own secret world.

Standing at the bay window of her living room, she gazed down onto the road bustling with buses, taxis, and private cars. Their horns filled the air as vehicles backed up into long traffic jams appropriate for this time of the night. Eventually, her eyes lifted from the chaos below directly into the flat opposite. Staring back at her was the tall stranger from Asraf's shop. As she stepped back from the window into the centre of the living room where she knew that only one pair of eyes could see her, she began to tremble with excitement. Instinctively, she knew the time was right and so she removed her jacket, letting it drop it to the floor. Her hands were trembling as she began to open her white blouse, slowly undoing it button by button and it too slid to the floor to reveal a silk and lace bra - startlingly white against her tanned body. Undoing the button on her trousers, she teased the zip down as far as it would go, before allowing them to fall to the floor, revealing the matching silk and lace thong. Standing there she felt the warm sensuality of revealing herself, while still in the safety of her own home. Stepping out of the crumpled trousers, she turned around and raised her arms behind her, unclipping the bra and slipping it off. She gazed over her shoulder and smiled as she left the room, pleased at the hunger in his eyes.

Her clothes for the evening had been selected in advance. The ebony coloured leather coat hung from its hanger, the belt ready to be cinched around her narrow waist. A crimson top and tight-fitting jeans lay on the bed, knee-high boots with spike heels stood on the bedroom floor. Donning her outfit she finished her ensemble with lipstick matching the red of her shirt and so the transformation from respected businesswoman to sultry and controlling vixen was complete. Once ready, Yvonne went downstairs and out onto Dumbarton Road, briefly glanced up at the flat opposite and nodded her head, walking along Dumbarton Road towards Partick Railway station. She knew that he was close behind her.

"Balloch, return please."

The assistant at the ticket counter exchanged the fare for her tickets and she proceeded to the westbound platform via the escalator while the subway trains thundered beneath her feet. Venturing out of the glass-enclosed waiting room onto the platform, she stood where the first carriage was likely to stop. The light on the signal changed to green as the train rolled into the station before coming to a halt. She boarded the train, drawing admiring glances from male passengers and jealous scowls from the females. She was magnetic, and the feeling of power excited her.

Stepping off the train at Balloch she looked around at the other passengers, then caught sight of one in particular. Heading out onto Balloch Road, she turned right and crossed the tracks before walking towards Drumkinnon Bay. She walked alone, but he was not far behind.

Standing at the edge of the River Leven, she watched the scarlet summer sun begin to set over Loch Lomond, painting the water blood-red. In the marina, small waves reduced into ripples that gently bobbed the anchored motorboats and yachts, welcoming her with soft and gentle splashes. To her right sat the old paddle steamer, the Lady of Loch Lomond, large circular paddles still and silent due to a lack of funds. It was doubtful she would ever again give passengers the nostalgic feeling of a bygone era.

Yvonne turned and slowly wandered along a curving pathway that had been carved out through the woods until she came across a familiar sight, the mouth of the fast-flowing River Leven. She gazed along the pathway, which was lined by large trees on both sides, their overhanging branches entwined like lovers, when her line of sight was drawn to a tall silhouetted figure with familiar piercing eyes watching her from the opposite bank. She made sure to remain within his line of vision as she took a few steps forward to stand at the water's edge. Directly across the way, a man was perched in front of a wooden easel, painting the peaceful scene of the Loch before him. Grey hair reached his shoulders, he wore a loose-fitting creme linen suit, and using the artist's brush in sweeping strokes he looked like a modern-day DaVinci or Rembrandt. Yvonne envied his ability to record the scene through his own artistic eyes.

As though in slow motion, she watched the paintbrush he used so confidently slip and fall to the ground, his suddenly limp body following, slipping gracefully down the embankment like a small craft being launched. He floated into the Loch where he would sink without a trace for possibly weeks, possibly months, possibly forever.

Yvonne sat on the train back to Partick, watching the world go by, her thoughts turning to her next adventure and still more excitement, and while walking back along Dumbarton Road under the tall streetlights, she feared no one; knowing she was not alone. Locking the door behind her once again, she was safely home. She went into the living room and switched on a small lamp, its orange bulb giving the room a warm glow.

Simultaneously a light came on in the flat opposite, attracting her attention. She saw her stranger. He saw her watching him. In reciprocation of their earlier game, he removed his leather coat, throwing it onto a nearby couch. Slowly, he removed all but one article of clothing revealing a chiselled, muscular body. She could see the bulge, letting her know that he was as excited as she was. Just as she had done to him, he turned around before removing the final under garment, revealing tight round buttocks. He switched off the light as he left the room.

Yvonne headed to bed. She could feel the sweat on her palms and her heart was pounding as if it was about to explode.

Chapter One

By day, Yvonne Duncan was an astute and successful businesswoman with an affluent yet unpretentious lifestyle. Having never been a spendthrift, her only flamboyant luxury in life was her annual holiday overseas. Her wardrobe was minimal but elegantly expensive, consisting mainly of tailored business suits and leisurewear, and as she was single and a loner she rarely ventured out, so only on occasion needed evening clothes. All her close friends were married and she seldom saw them. She paid the mortgage on her flat, and without a car she did not worry about the insurance. She was above average height, her large brown eyes contained golden flecks that sparkled in the sun, and her smile could dazzle and disarm. Her slim figure was honed by hours at the gym, and usually wore her flaming red hair swept back into a long ponytail. Now in her late thirties, she had dedicated much of her youth to building her publishing business so romance and marriage had never been at the forefront of her mind, and while relationships were few and far between she never lacked admirers.

Yvonne Duncan Publications was situated in the centre of Glasgow on the fourth floor of a traditional red sandstone building with tall chimneys and refurbished sash windows that overlooked Buchanan Street. Her modern, glass-panelled office gave her a clear view of her staff's activities; phone calls from potential authors and poets, arranging events at book fairs and festivals, and generally keeping the day-to-day workings of her publishing business running smoothly.

"Good morning," Yvonne greeted her staff promptly at nine o'clock.

They were already hard at work, critiquing submissions, proofreading, and editing books. As she glanced around the open office, she noticed that one staff member was missing from her desk.

"Guys, has anyone seen Anne this morning?"

Everyone looked around blankly just as the phone in Yvonne's office began to ring.

"Good morning, Yvonne Duncan speaking," she answered in the bright and cheery tone reserved for clients.

"Yvonne, it's Anne. I'm sorry but I can't come in today. I'm with my mum. My dad is missing. He hasn't been seen since last night." A deep, shuddering breath followed.

"Oh, Anne! I am so sorry to hear that. Do you know where he was? Have you called the police?"

Anne began to sob. "H-h-he loved going down to the Leven at this time of the year with his brushes and h-h-his easel. He adored painting the boats near where the Lady of Loch Lomond is moored."

The vision of a body slipping slowly into the Leven flashed vividly in Yvonne's mind as she consoled her assistant.

"Anne, is there anything I can do for you? Whatever it is, please let me know, and of course, keep in touch." The only response a whispered thanks and the gentle click of a phone disconnecting.

Yvonne slumped at her desk and wondered, *what are the chances of me witnessing the death of my assistant's father? What if there was a single, solitary witness who had seen me on the opposite side of the river and could identify me. Well, there is, but I have control of him.*

"Right guys, time to lock up for the weekend. Finish off what you're doing and let's meet at the local for a drink."

Looks flashed around the room as everyone thought the same thing. While the staff were used to Friday night drinks at their local, The Pub on the Square, they were not to having the boss accompany them, this was something new. Everyone knew that Yvonne kept her life outside of the office very private, not one to give up details of herself to her inquisitive staff.

They all rallied together and locked up the office for the weekend. As they wandered through George Square, chatting amongst themselves Yvonne let her thoughts drift. On her right-hand side was a series of up-scale restaurants, including her favourite chain, Green's. Rather than heading to a rowdy pub, it was one of these that Yvonne would much rather head into – gentle piano music drifting out of invisible speakers, plush carpets and expensive cocktails. She sighed quietly, rousing herself from her daydream and catching up to her staff.

After a couple of hours of socialising, 'the boss' decided it was time to catch the train back to Partick. She stood on the raised steps at the door of the pub, overlooking George Square with its white marble war memorial, statues of famous Scots and prim manicured gardens with wooden benches dotted around. For Yvonne, there was always something special about George Square, especially during the summer months when the sunset reflected on the grey sandstone of the looming city buildings. Tonight was the usual, bustling with people heading for the pubs after a week in the office, stag or hen nights starting to gather pace, individuals waiting at prearranged meeting points for girlfriends, boyfriends, or even a first date. Add the number of foreign tourists in the mix, and it all created a space for a people watcher to revel in. However, tonight, her only aim was to reach the sanctuary of her home on Dumbarton Road.

Yvonne let the weight of her body rest against the door after following the usual routine of securely locking it. Her briefcase fell to the floor, and she kicked her shoes off somewhat haphazardly, before compulsively placing them neatly beside her briefcase. Standing there in her stockinged feet for a moment, she sluggishly trudged into the living room. Just as she was about to turn on the small lamp, her eyes darted to the flat opposite in anticipation. It was in darkness. She suddenly drew back from the light switch, allowing only the subdued glow of the streetlights below to filter in. Alone in her flat, the 'other' Yvonne took over; the controller, the vixen, the outsider. She slipped out of her designer suit and into her seductive leather coat. Waiting for him, she sat in her wide-armed, soft, red, leather armchair facing across the road. The clock ticked time away, second by second, minute by minute, echoing the heartbeat that rang in her ears.

Eventually, a dim light crept into the living room across the road. She could see his silhouette in the doorway before the main light was switched on. She rose from her seat and approached the window until she felt that she could reach out and touch him he was so close. He looked into her flat, and wearing his deep navy-blue suit, white shirt and dark tie, he looked every inch a respectable businessman. But she knew better.

Her breath suddenly hitched in her throat as she saw a tall curvaceous brunette wearing a sultry violet evening dress enter the room and wrapping her arms around his waist. He tilted his head to rest against hers as they both looked out across the road. Yvonne coolly watched as his hand caressed her arm tenderly. The ticking of the clock was deafening as Yvonne contemplated her next move. The unknown woman was in front of her man reaching up to caress his jawline before slowly undoing his tie while his arms gently brushed down the deep plunge on the back of her dress until his hands reached her waist. He did not flinch as he held Yvonne's gaze.

Yvonne slammed the door behind her. Everyone in the stairwell heard it and the vibrations could be felt on the stairhead. As the echo in the close gradually subsided, families returned to normal – whatever the cause, they chose to ignore it.

Yvonne stormed up towards Byres Road, her fiery red hair matching her temper as it whipped around her face, and the long coat flapped with each step as she had been too agitated to carefully cinch it around her waist as she normally would. She was focused on her three-stage mission – locate, engage, destroy.

The shops and pubs on her left passed in a blur as she crossed Byres Road towards Church Street, without stopping. Having passed over the River Kelvin, she saw the imposing silhouette of the magnificent Grove Art Gallery and Museum, lit up to show off its imposing façade. This was one of her favourite places in Glasgow and it brought back fond memories of her childhood. She would wander around the building designed in a Spanish baroque style, finished with traditional Locharbriggs red sandstone. Even as a young girl visiting the gallery with her parents, she had marvelled at the huge mahogany and glass rotating doors at both entrances, which would loom over her tiny frame. The vast open foyer, marble floors and grand staircase, felt like the biggest space in the world. She always tried to take the stairs two at a time, and used to run along the corridor of the upper balcony for a closer view of the concert pipe organ that was installed almost one hundred and twenty years ago and her favourite object in the gallery. Even now she was a regular visitor and as years passed, she developed a deeper appreciation of the artwork housed within. The height of the spires across the length of the building was enough to ground her for a moment as she recalled her younger years.

She remembered how the stranger had slighted her and the fury reignited. Panting heavily, she stood at the entrance to Grove Park and scanned the area, which was unusually quiet for a Friday evening – then again, the university was closed for the summer holidays, so most of the students had returned home to their families.

Teenage mountain bikers were performing tricks for each other, and any spectators, on the purpose-built concrete bowl, with its undulating curves and sweeping bends allowing them to fly through the air with ease. Some of the landings were less than graceful as bike and rider were left sprawled on the concrete with only a helmet, elbow and knee pads preventing serious injuries. There were a few glances in her direction from the older teenagers as she slowly strolled towards them.

"Aw' right, missus, fancy a shot on ma bike?" Shouted one which was met by laughter from his friends.

"Haw you," yelled the oldest, "dinnae be cheeky tae the wummin. It's no' a bike she's wantin' tae ride!" The posse cheered and whooped as he flashed her a brazen grin.

She stood staring at each of their faces, her feet shoulder-width apart and hands deep in the pockets of her coat.

"You! What's your name?" She commanded.

"Mike, Mike the Bike, best ride you'll get," smirked the scruffy-haired teenager, his knees poking through the holes in his jeans.

"Really?" she countered with a sly smile. "Nice to have met you."

She turned her back on them and the boys watched as she wandered along the pathway that ran parallel to the River Kelvin until she was out of sight. She had achieved her objective quicker than she thought she would. Target located and engaged.

Hiking up the sloping path back onto Kelvin Way, she turned towards Sauchiehall Street and crossed the wide road, taking a shortcut through The Grove Art Gallery and Museum car park. A few cars left in parking bays, temporarily abandoned by their owners, nowhere to be seen.

Her walk home was more controlled and relaxed. There was a sense of satisfaction as she went up the stairs to her flat. This time, the door was closed quietly, so not to disturb the neighbours at two o'clock in the morning. She made a concerted effort to check the state of the flat across from her own - it was in darkness. She looked at the clock on the wall. The ticking was barely audible.

In the privacy of her bedroom, she draped her beloved coat on its hanger, while letting the rest of her clothing fall to the floor as she climbed into bed, naked and alone. Under the duvet, she curled into a foetal position which, ever since she was a small child, made her feel safe.

That night, she had trouble sleeping. A movie played and repeated behind her eyelids, it was the sight of 'Mike the Bike' hurtling down the grass embankment towards her. She could only guess that the boy spotted her and was hurtling towards her at a speed greater than his ability to control.

Daylight streamed in through her bedroom window and Yvonne awoke with a start. Slowly everything came back to her, her trek along the path, the bike flying towards her, the stranger who had pulled her out of harm's way. A stark vision of the bike and rider in the River Kelvin.

Surely not.

She turned on the bedside radio and lay impatiently waiting for the news. She felt a sense of relief when there was no mention of an incident or accident in the park.

Chapter Two

A week had passed since Anne broke the news of her father's disappearance and Yvonne decided that it was time to check in. She drummed her fingers on her desk until she heard the click of a receiver.

"Hi Anne, it's Yvonne. Any word about your dad?"

"No, nothing yet…" Anne expelled a shuddering sigh before continuing. "The police are talking about extending the search as they found his brushes and easel down on the banks of the Leven." Hiccuping sobs erupted from the other end of the phone.

In her gentlest tone, Yvonne tried to console her assistant. "I am so sorry, Anne. Do take as much time off as you need. I know how close you are, ehhh were to your father."

"Th- thanks. I know, and it's hard on my mum too, they have never been apart for a night since they married." One more ragged breath and Anne continued, "I promise I'll stay in touch."

At the end of the working day, Yvonne took her neatly packed kit bag and walked to the local gym on Dumbarton Road, where she met up with her trainer, Lorenzo, one of the very few men whom she had been seriously attracted to in all her life. He was twenty-seven, about six feet four inches tall, with jet-black wavy hair that swept down to his collar. Born in Sardinia, he had that swarthy Italian look about him, with deep-set brown eyes and tanned skin eerily reminiscent of the stranger who lived opposite her. Yvonne always marvelled at the fact that there was not a single ounce of fat on his muscular body.

As the sweat dripped down her face, stinging her eyes, Lorenzo demanded that little bit of extra effort before bringing the hour-long session to a halt. She collapsed over the handlebars of her spin bike, exhausted.

"To think… I pay you…. to do this… to… me," she panted, desperately trying to get air back into her lungs.

"Yes, and I thank you," he chuckled, while she dug around in her kit bag for his fee. "And you get to do it all again next week."

Having recovered slightly, she countered, "Thanks, Lorenzo. I'm shattered."

"Listen, it all takes time. What's it been, six weeks since you signed up?"

"Yes, something like that."

"Give it a few more weeks and you'll feel great, the same as you already look. Your husband is a lucky man." He eyed her up and down as if gauging her reaction.

"He would be if I was married," she quipped back.

"Oh, sorry, I just assumed," he stammered, looking abashed.

"Never assume anything in this life, Lorenzo." Yvonne gazed into his eyes, her subliminal message quite clear.

There was no doubt that Lorenzo was interested in her, but he was a professional with a reputation of never getting intimate or involved with his clients.

"Thank you, Yvonne, I'll remember that for the future," he acknowledged, maintaining their eye contact.

She broke away as she cleaned the bike. "What about you? Married, girlfriend, both?"

Laughing he responded. "Neither." He glanced at his watch. "Now I have my next appointment. Will I see you next week Yvonne?"

"Yes, Lorenzo, I'll be here."

"See you then," he called out over his shoulder as he headed over to the client patiently waiting at the door.

Yvonne emptied the contents of her bag onto the kitchen floor. In her usual fashion, the sweaty Lycra outfit went straight into the washing machine, while her trainers and bag went into the cupboard, ready for another week. She showered and put on a fresh outfit then sat at her dining table to log into her business account on her laptop. Next to the computer was a glass of Sauvignon Blanc and a large Greek salad for dinner.

Yvonne was active on all the social media sites that were linked to her company website. It was paying off as the traffic to her site increased daily, which was good news for potential clients. She poured over spreadsheets and figures provided by her accountants, her business was in a very healthy financial state and the future looked good.

Her thoughts turned to Lorenzo and his occupation. She did not have anyone on her books who had written a fitness training manual. Yes, the market was flooded with healthy living and personality-endorsed 'keep fit' books, but maybe Lorenzo could offer something different. Suddenly, her phone rang, jolting her back to reality.

"Hello?"

"Hello Yvonne, it's Lorenzo. I have a client who's cancelled tomorrow at one o'clock. He's already paid for the hour so would you like to take it? Free of charge, of course."

"Yes, that would be great, thank you! I actually have something to discuss with you, so I'll bring it up with you then."

"Oh, how intriguing. Maybe we can talk about that on the bike," he chuckled.

Later that evening, she sat browsing the home page of the local news. It announced that the police were preparing to send their underwater unit into Loch Lomond to search for the body of Anne's father. Her heart raced and sweat formed a thin cover on her palms. After trawling the web for more information, she found in a separate article that the body of a teenage boy had been recovered from the River Kelvin. Police had declined to name the deceased until relatives had been informed and a formal identification had taken place.

The two articles shook her.

She rose from her chair, drawn to the window and gazed as locals drifted from pub to pub. The working week was once again finished and everyone was ready to enjoy their weekend. Police officers were already out on beat patrol, chatting to youngsters who should have been heading home, but instead chose to hang about the street corners.

This is when she sometimes missed having a boyfriend, or a partner, or even a friend – just someone to share the weekend with. She decided to go out to a little place that she knew well. Going into her bedroom, she pulled on a simple sky-blue silk shirt, which she tucked into the waistband of a pair of skin-tight blue jeans. She slipped on her favourite pair of brown suede Chelsea boots, and the chocolate brown leather biker-jacket finished off her outfit. Looking into the mirror she decided to leave her hair down, shaking out her ponytail.

She settled into the quaint establishment known simply as The Café. Friday night had all the potential to be an enjoyable evening with music, and interesting company, as there was always somebody nearby to talk to.

As she sat alone with her back to the window, watching couples chatting, her thoughts turned once again to Anne and the kid found in the River Kelvin. Her emotions were tumultuous as the small four-piece band struck up, drowning out any attempts at a conversation with the person next to you, let alone across the table. That was the other thing that Yvonne loved about this little gem, hidden in the West End. There were no television screens to distract you – no football, no news channels, no subtitles, just a pub, a special pub with a band.

As her attention drifted between listening to the music and people-watching, she was aware of a woman and her companion making direct and unwanted advances to the man sitting at the bar, he was visibly uncomfortable with the attention he was getting. Yvonne rose from her table and took the few short steps over to him, sneaking up behind him before kissing his cheek.

"Hey, babe didn't you see me? I've got a table by the window," she purred into his ear.

"Oh sorry! No, I didn't!" Relieved to see a friendly and beautiful face as he moved over to join her. Lorenzo set his kitbag down on the floor and winked.

"Twice in one day," he said with a smile. "Oh, and thank you for rescuing me."

"We've still got tomorrow to come," she teased.

"Oh yes, my one o'clock."

"Lorenzo! is that all I am to you, your one o'clock?" she gasped, hand against her heart pretending to be offended.

A small smile played at the edge of his mouth.

"I should've left you with these two man-eaters." Yvonne pouted and crossed her arms for dramatic effect. "Anyway, what brings you in here?"

"Sometimes on my way home I drop in for a coffee and maybe a small liqueur, have a listen to the music, which I love. What about you?" He leaned forward, waiting in anticipation for her answer.

"I was sitting alone at home, but I didn't want to be. I love it here, so I came in for a coffee. But while you have the liqueur of your preference, I may just have a brandy."

Yvonne looked over Lorenzo's shoulder, his two admirers jealously staring. She raised her hand and summoned the waitress who was standing nearby. "One cognac liqueur and one brandy, please."

Lorenzo watched her intently. "You know, you're going to suffer for this tomorrow," he taunted.

"Well then, I'm in good hands" she replied, distracted still by his two admirers. They stood up, heading over to the ladies' toilets.

"Excuse me, Lorenzo."

Upon entering the toilets, she could hear them talking about the 'bitch with her boy toy' from inside a cubicle. She heard toilets being flushed, doors being unlocked, and thrown open in unison followed by the startled looks on their faces as they encountered 'the bitch'.

"Ladies, take my advice and leave," advised Yvonne, in a low menacing tone that shocked even her.

"Who dae you think you're talkin' to?" bristled the one with brassy blonde hair that was in dire need of care and attention. "Do you know who I am, bitch?"

"No, but I'm sure your carer has your name. Ask them if you can't remember it," Yvonne retorted flippantly.

"Whit?" replied the confused blonde.

"Think about it, babes," called Yvonne over her shoulder as she returned to Lorenzo.

"Everything okay?" He inquired as Yvonne sat down.

"It is now," she answered cryptically, staring at the toilet door. A golden brandy had materialised next to her empty coffee cup while she had been away.

"May I?" He gestured to the seat beside Yvonne. "I can see the band better from there."

Yvonne simply nodded as he moved to sit beside her, pulling his drinks across the table. At the same time, the two women emerged from the toilet. One was instructed to gather their jackets from their table, while the other approached Lorenzo.

"Haw pal, your girlfriend is a nutter, you should be careful around her."

"Now," said Lorenzo, "you're my girlfriend – when did that happen?"

"It happened when I rescued you from them. And listen, if I was about ten years younger, I would naturally be your girlfriend - if I wanted to." Yvonne felt powerful, in control, after her little victory. She could not help flirting.

"Well having looked at your file, you look a lot younger than your actual age."

"Thank you, Lorenzo, you are a darling." Yvonne giggled, batting her eyelashes.

"Tell me," he asked, "are you actually a nutter?"

"Oh, you have no idea how much of a nutter I can be," she quipped back, laughing.

The band continued to play as they listened to one song in companionable silence.

Lorenzo was the first to break it. "You said that you wanted to speak to me about something?"

"Yes, I do. It's an idea I've had. What do you know about me, Lorenzo?"

"Very little other than what's on your file. Name, age, date of birth and your home address."

"I'm a very private person. As you know I'm thirty-eight, no boyfriend, partner or husband." Yvonne paused. "The reason I am those things is that I've dedicated most of my working life to building my own publishing business. I have a small but dedicated staff, editors, proofreaders, etcetera, and of course my own personal assistant." She finished with a smile

"Right. Where do I fit into all this then?" he queried.

"Well, have you ever thought about writing a book on personal fitness?"

"No, never."

"Is it something that you would consider?"

"I can give it some thought, but I wouldn't know where to begin."

"That's why I'm here. With my team we'd be able to come up with something new and different, something unique to you, not the normal straightforward keep-fit."

"Okay, let me think about it. Now, can I ask you something?" probed Lorenzo.

"Depends on what it is. I might not answer."

"Can you tell me why you're single, other than building up your business?"

Yvonne was taken aback, unprepared for how bluntly his question had been delivered. "I've just never found Mr Right, or someone I want to share my life with."

She could feel heat spreading across her cheeks.

"Why are you blushing?" he teased.

"That's two questions, you said you only wanted to ask me one!" she shot back.

There was another brief pause because she ventured, "please tell me about my trainer?"

"Well, I was born in Sardinia, a whole twenty-seven years ago – I know, can you believe it, I'm ancient! – then, I was brought here when I was seven, I stayed for school and university, got my degree in English Literature, but academia was never my thing. I then qualified as a sports coach and personal trainer. I could never see myself sitting in an office day in and day out. My parents are still in Sardinia, and they've always been good to me. I have one sister, Maria, who's twenty-four and still at home."

"Do you live with anyone?" ventured Yvonne tentatively.

"That's another question, as you said to me." A devilish gleam was in his eye.

"Touché."

"I have my flat with a small area I keep aside for my reiki and massage therapy sessions."

"Brains and brawn then all rolled into one?" She arched one eyebrow as she asked the question.

"Oh, I wouldn't say that." He chuckled as they settled into an easy banter with one another.

"I would… So, why are you single?" came her loaded question.

"For exactly the same reasons as you, so we're alike there. I never get involved with clients, word spreads and your reputation is ruined because you've been chasing someone's wife or girlfriend. Thing is, I never get accused of chasing someone's boyfriend or husband." He winked and laughed.

"Wait, ahhhh…" she began before he hastily interrupted.

"No, defo' not, I like the ladies."

"Thank God for that," escaped before she realised what she had said, right as the band fell silent. She clapped a hand across her mouth before she said anything else. Her face was crimson, matching the colour of her hair.

"You're blushing again," he murmured with a smile.

"No wonder! Everyone in here must have heard me say that. Why does the band always stop when you're mid-sentence," she spluttered, laughing and leaning into Lorenzo, placing her hand on his thigh.

Realising what she'd done, she started to apologise, when Lorenzo interrupted, "Yvonne, it's fine, honestly."

"You sure?" Yvonne twirled a strand of her hair and stared intently at the table.

"Very sure," he whispered, gently tipping her chin up and gazing deeply into her eyes. Yvonne sat upright as she lifted her brandy glass, taking a sip, recovering from what she felt as an awkward moment.

They both began to speak at the same time, then they just laughed.

"Please, you first," he volunteered.

"Thank you."

"For what?"

"Being a gentleman, for a start. I can't remember the last time I had a good laugh like this and um…" she paused, trying to find the right words. "And, well, just me sitting here with someone that I know. I'm trying to find the right words to say. What am I trying to say? Do you know what I mean?"

"Well, as a book publisher, if I do ever write a book, you have no chance of getting it," he chuckled, nudging her with his shoulder.

"Smart-alec," she teased right back.

"Now, Yvonne – or should I call you Miss Duncan? To call your trainer a smart-alec is not a great idea when you've had a large brandy and a session booked for tomorrow."

"I wish I were ten years younger," she murmured.

"Age is only a number, Yvonne, never forget that," he murmured in return and finished his drink.

"Would you like another?" she invited tentatively. She enjoyed his company and was reluctant to be left alone so soon.

"No, thanks, I have to get going. Unlike you fancy 'business people' I'm on the bus home."

"Oh, what do you think us 'business people' drive then?" she taunted.

"Oh, BMW, Audi, Mercedes, whatever. Then again, nowadays it's probably a big four-wheel drive."

"Well I have a few drivers," she giggled. "A bus driver, a train driver and a subway driver!"

"See that woman earlier that said you were a nutter? I believe her." Lorenzo laughed with her, both knowing that her joke had been terrible, but that just made it all the more hilarious.

"Thank you so much for tonight, I've enjoyed it."

"Yeah, and me too with you," he agreed, picking up his bag. "See you tomorrow?"

"Yes, see you tomorrow, Lorenzo," she echoed as he left the bar.

Chapter Three

Yvonne sat alone once again and there was an emptiness deep inside her. Slowly, the contents of her glass began to circle round and round as she twirled it in her hand. Even the sound of the band playing could not distract her. Memories drifted back to the time her parent's died, the drunk driver hit their car head on, they died instantly. She remembered the emptiness it left, how pleased she was knowing he died too. She was fourteen, and that single incident changed her forever.

As she continued to sit and reflect her mind drifted to Lorenzo. It was crazy to think for a split second that he would be interested in someone ten years his senior and so wrapped up in her business that she would have no time for him. She downed the rest of her drink in a rare moment of self-pity.

Out the corner of her eye, she saw a sports bag being thrown onto the floor which distracted her from her thoughts, but she made a point of not looking up.

"Would you like another drink, and maybe some company?" asked Lorenzo, who had materialised above her.

"Yes please," she responded smiling and confident, while in her head she was frantically repeating to herself stay calm, stay calm, over and over again.

He slid into the chair and beckoned the waitress over to order another drink.

"What brings you back here?" she inquired, her pulse quickening with him sitting so close to her again – she could smell his aftershave.

"I missed my bus."

"You missed your bus?" she echoed incredulously. "Every bus that passes through here goes into the city."

"Really? My mum never told me that," he teased. "I came back to hear the rest of this band's set, I like them." His fingers were tapping his thigh in time with the music as if to prove his point, while his eyes were solely locked on her.

"Is that all that you liked in here tonight?" she quizzed, unable to meet his gaze.

"To be honest, no."

When he didn't offer any more information, Yvonne pushed for it. "Would you like to expand on that answer?"

"I came back because of the company I was with."

After a brief pause, he tripped over the rest of his answer, as if he could not get it out quickly enough. "The lady I was sitting with is seriously attractive and the fact that she's single is very appealing. I would hate to lose her to someone else, just because I got on a bus. Then again, I don't even know if she's interested but I had to take the chance that she just might be. Does all that make sense to you?"

He was rambling and she thought it was quite cute. "Yes, it does," she stated gently, raising her eyes to meet his.

"While I'm on a roll, would you like to go out for dinner with me?"

Her heart ached. This was exactly what she had wanted to hear, but she had to be sure that it was also what he wanted. "Lorenzo, don't take this the wrong way, but I am old enough to be…"

He interjected before she could finish. "Who? My older sister? Certainly not my mother."

"I don't do dating, Lorenzo," she retaliated, going on the defensive.

Disappointment flashed across his face as his lips tightened and he shrugged his shoulders, and the ache in her heart returned.

"Lorenzo, I am sorry. I truly am."

"Hey, all good, personal trainer and client, strictly a professional relationship, it's good that way." It was now Lorenzo's turn to be defensive. He stood up from the table and slung his bag. "I should go. See you tomorrow?"

"Yes, see you tomorrow," a sad echo in her voice.

Yvonne's eyes followed him as he walked back into the night. Then as she lifted her drink, her eyes met those of a woman staring at her from across the room. She was sitting with her partner, neither of them were speaking to each other, both more interested in what was happening in the land of social media. She shook her head from side to side in a not-so-subtle signal of disapproval, as she had noticed the look of disappointment on Lorenzo's face, and the look upon Yvonne's face, the one that said she had sadly let him leave alone.

It was all the encouragement she needed.

Yvonne lifted her glass and the remainder of the brandy slid down her throat as easily as she rose from the table, much to the delight of the smiling stranger, who slammed her glass on the table in solidarity and excitement.

She saw a city-bound bus about to turn onto the Thornwood roundabout from Scotstoun, she looked left, the bus stop was about one hundred yards away and there was no way that she was going to make it there before the bus. Yvonne did not even know if Lorenzo was there, although a few people were milling about at the bus stop she could not help but hope. Looking back through the window into the pub, she saw the lady nod to her, as if to say, yes, go get him. Yvonne grinned and started running as the bus crept past her.

She watched as the last of the passengers boarded, the doors hissing shut behind them. She could only yell obscenities in her head as the bus drew away heading for the city. She leaned over, placing her hands on her knees and shaking her head, gasping. While catching her breath, her phone started ringing from one of her pockets and as she stood and pulled it from her pocket Lorenzo's name showed as the caller .

"Lorenzo!" she panted.

"We have to work on your fitness," he laughed from the other end of the line.

"What do you mean?" she scoffed, pretending to be offended.

"Well, there you are, absolutely knackered from a brisk walk from the pub towards the bus stop."

"Where are you?" she demanded, looking bewilderedly around her, trying to spot him in the dark.

"Opposite you, Yvonne. Did you honestly think I was going to give up that easily on taking you out for dinner?"

"I suppose I didn't give you much encouragement, did I?" She conceded, spotting him standing a short distance away. They simply stared at each other, all the while continuing the conversation through their phones.

"No, but never underestimate a male with Italian blood in his veins."

"Okay. Tell me something before you hang up?"

"Would it bother you seeing a woman ten years older than you?"

Lorenzo hung up and walked slowly towards her, before speaking to her directly. He lifted her chin up towards him and expressed all of his feelings sincerely. "I do not see a woman ten years older than I am. I see a beautiful woman with stunning eyes, a beautiful smile and the most gorgeous red hair I have ever seen in my life. Also, I just had the best night that I've had in many years. You make me laugh, Yvonne. I have never made an exception to my no-socialising with clients rule - you are one that I am going to make an exception for - the one I am going to break my own rule for." He hesitated a moment then continued. "Now, you tell me this… do you have a problem seeing a guy ten years younger than you?" he mocked impishly, the corners of his mouth lifting into a grin.

Yvonne's arms hung limply by her side, she was enamoured and could not tear her eyes away from him, so it took a moment before she could answer.

"I don't know. I've never been in this position before, to be honest. I rarely date, I don't even go out often, far less with someone younger than I am."

"Well, do you want to give it a go and see where it leads us?"

"Um… yes, that would be nice," Yvonne agreed hesitantly, as a smile broke out across her face.

Lorenzo's beaming grin matched her own. "Here comes my bus. I'll see you tomorrow."

"Do I get a kiss before you go?" she blurted.

"Hell no, we have to have a date first," he called over his shoulder as he swiftly passed her to get back to the bus stop.

She walked back to the pub in a state of euphoria. She ordered a large brandy as she sat back down. A pair of eyes were set firmly on her, and she nodded in euphoria, the woman returned a knowing smile.

As she strolled along Dumbarton Road, two women emerged from the shadows, bristling with hostility.

"Haw hen, where's yer toy boy? Away wae a younger burd?" shouted the brassy blonde.

"She's no fit enough for him, that's for sure," cackled the other.

Yvonne could feel her blood starting to boil, but this time something was holding her back. She just shook her head and walked away.

Just as she got into her flat, she felt her phone vibrate in her pocket. One new message. She scanned her fingerprint and the text read:

> *Looking forward to seeing you at one o'clock. Goodnight,*
> *sweet dreams, L xxx.*

The thought of seeing Lorenzo again so soon set a million butterflies off in her stomach, but she was also filled with trepidation about the secret life she led. She had only known this man for six weeks, so it would be easy to drop him like a stone. There was always the reliable excuse of workload, but she could not shake the feeling that this was different. She had to face that was attracted to him like no other man before.

"Right, Yvonne, get yourself in here and join the others." Lorenzo dictated as she arrived at the gym, in a room that was filled with a variety of fitness equipment.

A small group of people were milling about, waiting for the class to start. Yvonne dropped her bag near the door ensuring her water bottle was easily accessible. She was suddenly self-conscious with so many people looking at her. Lorenzo did not give her much time to fixate on that fact.

"Usual round of warm-up exercises, to begin with, let's go," he barked.

These consisted of eighteen Qigong movements, loosening and warming up their muscles. Thereafter, she was put onto the spin bike.

"Let's get those legs going, five minutes, remember to breath," he instructed, pushing everyone to their limits. "Okay, two minutes recovery time."

He walked around the room, checking in on how everyone was coping with their various exercises as they rotated around the stations.

Reaching Yvonne he whispered, "Someone was on the brandy last night. I can tell."

She grimaced in agreement but was determined to push herself harder and win this little game.

Five minutes later, Lorenzo called out across the room. "Stop, stop, stop. Everyone, go and take a break, get some water."

Yvonne staggered off the bike, her legs feeling like jelly and only just supporting her weight. A tiny blonde woman with bright green eyes and about the same age as Yvonne suddenly appeared at her side introducing herself as Gillian in an annoyingly bubbly tone.

"Hello, Gillian. I'm Yvonne."

"Not seen you here before on a Sunday."

"Yes, and not likely to again at this rate," joked Yvonne. She drank deeply to try and cool herself down.

"Honestly, he is amazing, worth every penny." Gillian was gawking at Lorenzo, making no attempt to hide her attraction. "Normally we do a one-to-one, but Sunday is a group session, and you can get competitive with others in the room. It's fun."

"You do one-to-one as in a private session with him?" interrogated Yvonne as she began to look Gillian up and down. "Do I detect a little bit of 'oh, I fancy him' somewhere in there?"

"Geez, you'd need to be an alien to not fancy him!" exclaimed Gillian, rolling her eyes. "But I'll tell you something. As long as you're his client, you have no chance, some rule he has that he won't break, and believe me, I've tried to make him break it."

"I guess there is no chance for me there at all then." Yvonne tried not to smile and then decided she was done with this conversation.

"Right everyone, if you're finished chatting, we can start again," yelled Lorenzo from across the room. "Bench presses. Find your weights, get pumping. Yvonne, with me, please. This is your first day, so I'll show you what to do."

He took her over to the equipment and began to talk her through it laying on the bench to demonstrate the technique. She appreciated the opportunity to watch his biceps as he went through the movement.

The end of the session was marked by his booming instruction. "Okay, five minutes left, then we'll cool down with some gentle stretches. After that, shower rooms, please. Thank you all for coming."

Lorenzo watched as Yvonne and Gillian trooped out of the room together, heading for the ladies changing room.

On their way, Gillian asked, "Will I see you again next Sunday? It's good to have another girl in the class."

"Oh, I don't know about that." Yvonne was reluctant to spend time with someone who was clearly trying to get a piece of Lorenzo.

"I'm going to ask Lorenzo then. I want a girly pal in the room," she laughed.

"Oh, well, I suppose you can ask."

Showered and changed, Yvonne walked into the cafeteria. Two cappuccinos lay on the small round table one for Lorenzo, and one waiting for her.

"Is it common practice to offer your new clients coffee on a Sunday?" she chided as she slid into an empty chair.

"Depends on who they are. How are you feeling after that?"

"Surprisingly good at the moment."

He did not reply, distracted by the television screen behind Yvonne.

"What are you watching?" She turned around to get a better idea of what was grabbing his attention. A news anchor was on screen.

"Hang on a minute, this is a shame." Lorenzo recapped what had already been said, about a kid named Michael Bradley found in the River Kelvin. "He was only eighteen. Police are trying to trace a woman who was seen in the area around the time Michael went missing. Sorry, you were saying?"

All the blood had drained from her face when she turned back around.

"Yvonne, are you okay?"

"Yes, sorry, yes I'm fine," she remarked automatically as she tried to compose herself. *No one knows you were there, it's fine.*

Slightly perturbed by her emotional response to the news, Lorenzo decided to change the subject. "Do you like Indian?"

"Are you asking me out on a date?"

"Yes, I am. You do know a refusal will put you at the back of the queue of waiting wenches," attempting to banter with her.

It worked. Since she did enjoy his company she felt her pulse begin to slow and she relaxed. "Well in that case, how can I refuse?"

His face lit up with joy. "So, is that a yes?"

"Yes," she echoed smiling back.

He pulled out his phone not taking his eyes off her.

"Hiya. Lorenzo Maldini here. Can I have a table for two, please? Eight o'clock tonight, and can I have one away from direct public view?"

He waited while a tinny voice confirmed all his details. "Thank you, brilliant. I knew I could trust you. See you at eight."

"Listen, Lorenzo, this is going at one hundred miles an hour and I am just a little nervous. I'm so not used to…" Yvonne hesitated.

"Well, welcome to Lorenzo's world. It's been a long time since Lorenzo did this for a wonderful woman. You are very special." He took her hand and squeezed it reassuringly.

"Hey Yvonne," came a call from the side, "you up for next Sunday?"

Yvonne quickly yanked her hand away before answering. "Will need to empty my piggy bank, Gillian, but hopefully."

"Great, see you then! Talk him into a discount," she smirked as she left the building.

Lorenzo's eyebrows raised at their exchange, but he did not question it. "Okay, back to where we were – can I pick you up at your place tonight?"

"Yes, that would be nice."

"Dress code – formal or casual?"

"How about casual, but smart?" she countered.

"Perfect," he grinned. "Shall we meet at, oh say, seven?"

"Yes, great!" She was beaming, feeling quite giddy just like a young girl on her first date, while desperately trying to remain relaxed and not let it show.

"So, what are you doing now, Lorenzo?"

"Me? Going home and chilling out, then I've got to get ready for a hot date tonight. What about you?"

"I got a guy picking me up tonight and I think that I am head over heels for him. Uh-oh! Tell me I did not just say that out loud?"

"Yes, you did, and I feel like that about her as well." He agreed which was comforting.

They picked up their bags and strolled outside in companionable silence.

"Until tonight then, Miss Duncan."

She wanted to make a comment about their age difference, just to be completely sure that he really liked her. She met his eyes, and knew at that moment that she did not need to ask, as they conveyed his complete attraction to her, assuring her that she never had to be insecure about the age difference between them.

"May I ask you something, Lorenzo?"

"Sure."

"May I have a kiss? I mean a real one."

"Thought you'd never ask," he beamed, taking her in his arms and kissing her gently on the lips.

"See you later," she whispered, breathless and ecstatic.

As she walked back to her flat, her mood was dampened slightly as the image of Michael Bradley hurtling down the grass embankment towards her popped into her head. Then there was the issue of the police divers heading for the River Leven.

Chapter Four

Yvonne stood in front of her full-length mirror, admiring her outfit. *Decidedly smart but casual*, she thought to herself. A pure white silk blouse, black jeans, blood-red short leather jacket, and red sling-backs with a small heel completed her look. Her long red hair was curled and left loose to hang over her shoulders. A light blush across her cheeks and a flick of mascara were all that she opted for in the way of makeup. The whole combination gave her a smouldering look that she hoped Lorenzo would like.

As the clock ticked towards seven o'clock, her heart had a strong but quick beat in anticipation of the evening. She did hope he that he would show up on time, if there was one thing that would put her off, it was someone being late – even if that someone was Lorenzo.

At six fifty-nine there was a knock at the door. She took a deep breath thinking, *this is it,*. She opened the door to see Lorenzo standing there in a pair of blue Armani jeans, a white shirt and a midnight blue waistcoat with a matching jacket. His black boots were so highly polished that she could see her reflection staring back at her. He carried a large bouquet of red roses which he held out to her, enticing her with his seductive smile.

As she took the roses from him her blush matched the vivid colour. "They're stunning, thank you so much!" Then she bent her head to breathe in the lovely fragrance.

"Yvonne?" he asked, interrupting her reverie.

"Yes?" She was still gazing at her gorgeous bouquet.

"Can I get an invite in, please, or am I just going to stand here?"

She dissolved into a fit of laughter "Yes, come in. Please, sit down. May I offer you a drink?"

"No thanks, I'm driving."

"What do you mean, driving?" she queried.

"You know, like in driving a car, four wheels, steering and all that," he kidded.

"Oh right, okay." She grappled with this information. She thought he only used public transport. "I'll put these into water. They're beautiful honestly."

Lorenzo reached out, taking her one free hand in his as she made a move to the kitchen. "Not nearly as beautiful as you. You look stunning, Yvonne."

"Thank you," she murmured as her heart began beating faster. *How does he do this to me?*

"I hate being late anywhere, so shall we head for dinner?" he asked, distracting her from her pounding heart.

Knowing that he shared her main pet peeve attracted her to him even more. She could not wait to spend this evening with him. "Yes, absolutely. Just give me a moment to put them in water."

In less than two minutes the red roses were in a crystal vase in the centre of the living room. Once she finished arranging them she walked over to Lorenzo, and wrapping her arms around his neck kissed him as she had never kissed anyone before. Her whole body was tingling from head to toe as she pressed herself closer to him. They slowly drew apart, unwilling to let go of each other quite yet, but aware of their approaching reservation.

"By the way, where's your car?"

"On the road outside. I couldn't get it up the stairs," he teased.

Yvonne glared at him mockingly, until she broke into a fit of giggles as she locked the door and they headed downstairs.

"Here," he said pointing towards a black Range Rover Sport, only a few months old, once they had made it out to the road.

"Really?" Yvonne stopped briefly in her tracks to stare at the monster vehicle.

"Yeah, really." He grinned as he opened the passenger door for her.

Stepping into the vehicle, she observed all the trappings of a top-of-the-range vehicle. Even with a successful company, this was something she could not afford.

"Think I'm in the wrong business," she sighed, more to herself than to him. However, he overheard her comment, and responded with a chuckle and a squeeze of her hand, before starting the ignition.

Turning into Church Street just off Dumbarton Road, he confidently pulled up outside the Kashmiri Cafe. Yvonne was searching for a parking spot when Lorenzo cut the engine.

"Um, Lorenzo… there are 'no parking' cones here."

"Yeah, I know, they're for us," he explained nonchalantly.

"Right," she conceded, impressed and confused, but unwilling to question the matter further. She undid her seat belt as he jumped out of the car and hurried to the passenger door to let her out.

"Do you know something, Mr Maldini? You are a gentleman."

She took his hand as she also slid gracefully out of the car. As they entered the restaurant it appeared almost every table was occupied. A young Indian man about five foot six, slimly built with short black hair slicked against his scalp, made his way over to them, arms open in greeting.

"Lorenzo, great to see you again my friend," greeted their host enthusiastically, a slight Glaswegian accent tinging his voice.

As they shook hands he inquired. "And who may this be?" His attention diverted to Yvonne, who had planted herself firmly beside Lorenzo.

"Ashi, this is Yvonne Duncan."

"I am so pleased to meet you," Ashi was shaking her hand just as enthusiastically as he had taken Lorenzo's.

"Lorenzo, she is beautiful my friend."

"Yeah, I know." Yvonne noticed that he could not help but smile.

"Is this where he brings all his first dates?" she probed jokingly.

Ashi looked confused and glanced between the two of them. "Lorenzo? He is rarely seen with a woman. He is so fussy."

Reassured, Yvonne slipped her hand into his.

"Right, please follow me, your table is ready just as requested."

Ashi led them to the rear of the restaurant, where he had set a table away from the main floor. "May I bring you some drinks?"

Yvonne thought about it for a moment. "A glass of red wine, please. Do you have a Cabernet?"

"Certainly, anything else?" He had no use for a notepad, simply memorising their orders.

"Yes, and a jug of iced water please."

"Oh, are you driving, Lorenzo? Which car did you bring your lovely date in, the Range Rover or the Ferrari?"

"The Range Rover tonight, Ashi," he laughed, looking somewhat abashed.

Yvonne looked between the two of them. "You have another car?"

"Oh yes, he has a red Ferrari!" Ashi exclaimed. "I am surprised he didn't use that on the first date to impress you."

Unaware of the magnitude of what he had just revealed, Ashi handed each of them a menu. "I shall go get your drinks, and I shall bring your favourite Pellegrino for you Lorenzo since you are driving."

"A Ferrari? And red." Yvonne arched one eyebrow in a questioning look which Lorenzo was careful to ignore and then shrugged as their server approached the table.

Yvonne took this this moment to glance around the restaurant with its deep red wallpaper and gold embossed designs. Large chandeliers hung from the ceiling dimly lit giving the restaurant a beautiful calm atmosphere for diners. High backed chairs surrounded the many tables. Abstract paintings adorned the walls. No expense was spared in keeping the restaurant number one in Glasgow.

"Good evening, may I take your order?" asked the waitress, digital notepad in hand to send their order directly to the chefs. They lifted their menus and glanced at what was on offer. Yvonne looked at Lorenzo and asked what he recommended.

"If you like fish I highly recommend the Tandoori Salmon starter, followed by, Murgh Makhani which is butter chicken, it is so soft and tender, or Goan Fish Curry, I love that."

Yvonne almost moaned aloud at the description, then decided. "May I have the salmon starter and butter chicken. Also, may I have a small glass of white Burgundy with my starter."

Yvonne caught Lorenzo's glance. "It is a perfect accompaniment with salmon."

"I will have to try a small one also since I am also ordering the salmon starter, but the Goan Fish Curry for my main course and then we must both have to finish with the strawberries and ice cream." Lorenzo winked and added to Yvonne, "but this ordinarily plain dessert is served with a twist that is only done in here."

After they placed their orders, Ashi returned with their drinks and wishing them a pleasant evening reminded them to find him should they need anything at all.

As the evening wore on, the attraction between Yvonne and Lorenzo grew deeper. Although this was their first date, it was as if they had known each other for years. They laughed and gradually shifted closer to one another until their legs were touching.

After a brief lull in the conversation, Yvonne acknowledged Lorenzo's commitment with a simple, "Thank you."

"For what?" Lorenzo asked, taking her hand.

"For not giving up on me last night."

"I was never going to give up on you. One way or another I was going to get you. You are a not only a beautiful woman, Yvonne Duncan, you also intelligent, funny, and I believe there is a mischievous side to you. So, I simply had to have you."

She ran her hands through her hair as she tilted her head back, disrupting the curls she had so carefully sculpted.

"Right, so now my turn. As I told you, I've not been out with anyone for a very long time, because as you know, I've poured myself into my business to make it a success. I've sacrificed a busy social life, I have a few good friends and try to spend some time with them. Though, to be honest my life recently is a bit of a mess." She waved away his inquiring look and continued, "then suddenly you turn up and I fall head over heels…"

Her voice trailed off into nothing as she realised she was about to say that she loved him. He was staring at her intently, so she had to continue. "I've haven't known what it's like to be in love for a very very long time, and while it's scary I like it."

She stared at Lorenzo trying to read his expression then finally asked. "So what have you got to say for yourself?"

"Well, first of all, I'm glad I got us a private table away from everyone." A slight smile played around the corners of his mouth. "Secondly when you came to me, what was it? Six weeks ago? The first time I saw you, I tried to treat you like you were just another client. But, I knew there was something quite special about you. If there was one client that I looked forward to seeing each week, it was you. Finally, as I said in the pub, I never mix business with pleasure. I can assure you, being with you is all pleasure. This is a first for me and I want to be with you, Yvonne Duncan."

He gazed at her so affectionately she wanted to kiss him right then and there.

"Does that mean I'm no longer your client?"

"As of right now. Now please tell me whether we are together or not?"

She could only smile. "I would love to be with you."

"It looks like you're going to need to find yourself another personal trainer," he quipped, the remark accompanied with a devilishly handsome grin. His eyes sparkled with contentment.

Yvonne looked at him smiled and nodded. "May I ask a question?"

"Sure, go for it."

"Do you really own a Ferrari?"

Lorenzo looked at her, tapping his finger on the table, debating what he wanted to say to her. As Yvonne sat looking at him, her mind was racing, and she just had to know.

"Please don't take this the wrong way," she began, "but you're a personal trainer, right?"

"Yes."

"And you got the bus home last night, but tonight you turn up tonight looking a million dollars in a Range Rover Sport, right?"

"Yes."

"Then Ashi tells me you own a Ferrari?"

"Correct again."

"And you have a flat in the city centre, right?"

"In Merchant City."

That answer took her by surprise. Exasperated by his blunt answers, Yvonne continued with her probing. "You have all that at twenty-eight and you don't have a girlfriend? Why is that?"

"Well, I didn't have a girlfriend before tonight, but I think I have one now," his thumb caressed her finger as they were locked together across the table.

"Can you understand where I'm coming from here?" she asked softly, looking him in the eyes. She was not going to let him avoid answering her.

"Yes," he replied gently. "You had to consider that I may be a gold digger, who's only after an older female with her own business and flat that I can leech off."

"Well, yes. For me trust is complicated, and that is why I rarely go out with anyone except friends."

She took a brief pause as she collected her thoughts. "Wait a minute. Did you say Merchant City?" The significance of the location suddenly dawned on her.

"Yes."

"Something is not adding up in all this."

"What's not adding up?"

Suddenly they were interrupted as Ashi came over to take their dishes away.

"Well, Lorenzo, how was your dinner?" inquired Ashi. "And, more important will you be going on a second date?"

"I haven't asked her yet, Ashi. I'm getting the third degree here at the moment."

Ashi was undeterred. "What about you, Yvonne? If you stick by my friend, you'll be the happiest woman in Glasgow."

"Is that right, Ashi?" She was beginning to feel sure, but she could not make it too easy for Lorenzo. She was enjoying toying with him.

"Yes, listen to me…" Ashi began.

"Ashi, shut it," interrupted Lorenzo sharply, beginning to get irritated.

"No, Lorenzo, my friend, the beautiful lady needs to hear this." Ashi turned to face Yvonne directly before he started speaking again. "Do you know after he booked this table for you both, he called me back and he said, 'Ashi, I've met someone special, really special, so make sure everything tonight is bang on.'"

"Thanks, Ashi. For that you are now my former friend," Lorenzo growled, flushing with embarrassment.

"Well it's true, he's infatuated, I can see it in his eyes. I have never seen that look before in him."

Yvonne redirected her attention to Lorenzo, who now resembled a ripe tomato. "Well, Mr Maldini, how are you getting out of that one?"

She grinned as she teased him to show him that the feeling was reciprocated.

"I guess I can't deny it. I did and I am." Clearing his throat in a feeble attempt to hide his embarrassment, he asked Ashi for the bill.

"Yes, of course," Ashi did not try to hide the enigmatic smile, as he walked away knowing he had achieved his objective of getting Lorenzo to admit his feelings for Yvonne.

As they were leaving Ashi waited for them by the door, his eyes alight with joy. "So, Yvonne, is he getting a second date?"

"I have to think about that, to be honest. But I'll be back here, dinner was fantastic! Honestly, that has been the best meal I've had in a long, long time."

He dipped his head slightly in gratitude. "So, he is seeing you again?" he probed once again.

"Maybe." Then she dazzled Ashi with a smile as she wrapped her arm around Lorenzo's waist.

"Ashi, you are a nightmare," commented Lorenzo. "Next time I'm going to a local takeaway."

"Yes, sure you are. Do you think you will get parked there?" he joked.

There was a round of handshaking as they all wished each other well, acknowledging a new friendship being forged.

"What time is it?" Lorenzo asked as they headed for the cool night air.

She checked her watch. "Just coming up on eleven."

"Okay, let's go," he said, swinging the Range Rover around then heading for the city centre along Dumbarton Road and Argyle Street.

They drew into Merchant City and Lorenzo pointed out his apartment building. The blond sandstone exterior was in pristine condition, recently restored. Originally built in the eighteen-hundreds the building stood three storeys high, understated almost modest but one of the most expensive residences.

Lorenzo swung the vehicle around, its headlights illuminating a pair of heavy, wrought-iron security gates, which opened with the push of a button on his key fob. He slowly drove down the ramp into a car park underneath the flats before parking in his reserved bay, while the gates slid quietly shut.

Lorenzo was quick to open the door and as Yvonne got out, she viewed the extravagance of the vehicles in the car park. There was more than a small fortune in expensive cars parked up here, secure from prying eyes, with the flashiest being a red Ferrari, parked in a corner. The number plate read LM 1.

"Come on, or everywhere will be closing," he said as he hurried her along.

"Where are we going?"

"Out to play for a little while."

Just who is this guy? she wondered to herself.

Chapter Five

As they stood at the entrance to the building, Lorenzo produced a card from his wallet which he held against a scanner opening the door automatically. They walked the short distance to the lift which then took them to the third floor. As the lift doors opened, Yvonne was met by a long hallway of gleaming white doors with gold numbers on them. They stopped at 3/3 with the name 'Maldini' on it, which was also security-card operated. Yvonne noticed a three-hundred-and-sixty-degree security camera watching their every move.

I wonder who else lives here as they clearly take building security seriously.

"Please, come in," gestured Lorenzo, holding the door open for her. The lights in the hallway burst into life as they stepped over the threshold, hidden sensors detecting their presence.

"Thank you." Her scan took in the large living room, with a high ceiling and carved cornices. It was huge and gorgeous, and it took her breath away. How could he afford to live like this?

"This is stunning…simply stunning." Her tone was admiring and she retained her calm as she did not want to sound unworldly or unsophisticated regarding the wealth before her.

"It's just an apartment," he replied in a cool calm tone. "Please, take a seat and I'll pour us a drink, then we'll go out for a little while."

Kicking off her shoes, then quickly setting them meticulously in the hallway just as she would at home, Yvonne sank into a luxurious, three-seater leather settee with matching seats across from her, the deep burgundy enhanced by the bright, clean white walls creating a juxtaposition of colour. Her eyes drifted around the room with the rest of its high-end modern furniture, a few Capo Di Monte figures were scattered around added to the elegance. Contrasting was a large fifty-inch Fulsen and Company

TV screen attached to the wall, matching DVD player with speakers, and on a glass stand lay more Fulsen and Company equipment. Under the television stood a marble mantlepiece, a large photograph graced the centre at its focal point. Nestled amongst other individuals in the photograph she immediately recognised Lorenzo. He handed her a glass of Rossa Toscana, which was the same shade as the settee.

"That's a beautiful photograph, Lorenzo."

"Thank you. That is *mia madre, mio padre, e mia sorella* – my mother, my father, and my sister." His eyes softened as his thoughts turned to his family, and her heart skipped a beat at seeing him vulnerable like this, so she decided to change the subject for him.

"This room is stunning, Lorenzo you have wonderful taste."

"Thank you. Come on, I'll give you a tour of the rest of the place." He pulled her up from her seat and placing his hand carefully on her waist, as if afraid to break her, he guided her out of the living room.

He opened a door and flipped on a light switch. "Okay, this is my room. Thankfully I tidied it today and changed the sheets. The lights in here are not movement activated, otherwise they would go on and off all night."

A large double bed with a deep blue silk duvet and matching pillowcases nestled between two bespoke bedside cabinets, topped with modern stainless steel lamps. A large mirrored wardrobe with sliding doors ran floor-to-ceiling and wall-to-wall, giving the illusion that space was double its actual size. There was minimal clutter and the only decoration was a stack of car magazines on the left bedside table. The deep pile carpet was dazzlingly white, and her senses were tingling with the luxury of the space.

"Oh, someone's confident." Smiling, Yvonne playfully nudged him with her elbow.

"Thanks." Lorenzo's trademark impish grin playing around the corners of his mouth as he turned off the light. "Now, depending on what you want to do later, either stay over or go home, this is my guest room."

The room he revealed reflected his bedroom, just a touch more simplistic as it contained a double bed, and the duvet was a muted taupe colour. The guest bedroom then led into another little room as Yvonne wondered, *how many rooms does this place have?*

"This room is my treatment, massage, and reiki room for personal clients who wish to remain, let's say... out of the public eye. And, last but not least, the bathroom."

To Yvonne it resembled something from a decorating magazine, with a central circular shower, a double basin with a bright back-lit mirror stretching across the sinks behind it. The walls and floor were decorated with marbled Italian tiles, once again expensive elegance. It was all so modern and she could completely imagine the two of them in that shower together.

Lorenzo looked at his watch and said, "Hey, I hate to cut the tour short, but shall we go?"

He led her out, gently intertwining his fingers together with hers.

Rounding the corner, they walked down Albion Street and reached Club Arthur where there was a long queue of restless people waiting to get into the popular music bar. Yvonne hated queuing and dreaded the thought of waiting to get in. Lorenzo, however, did not share her reluctance and walked right up to the security guard.

"Good evening, Mr Maldini," greeted the big burly bouncer at the door immaculate in his dark blue suit, white shirt and company monogrammed tie. He unhooked the queue management rope providing Lorenzo and Yvonne instant access. "I see you have company tonight."

"Good evening, Iain. How are you? And yes, this is Yvonne." Lorenzo pulled Yvonne in closer to him as he introduced her.

"Very good sir. See you on Wednesday, as usual?"

"Definitely Iain, the usual time," Lorenzo confirmed as Iain re-clipped the rope onto the chrome stand.

Holding hands, Lorenzo and Yvonne followed the stairs down below street level into the club with low lights and packed tables. A small LED dance floor was full of girls grinding against each other while their male partners stood chatting and drinking around the bar. This club was foreign to Yvonne which would normally make her wary, but with Lorenzo she felt safe. It was a world away from her own special Café that she loved so much, but she was happy to be out with Lorenzo.

As they curved their way through the throng, stopping to shake hands with numerous people, she was quick to realise that her date was a well-known and popular figure in the lively Glasgow scene, and that all eyes seemed to be on her by association.

Picking up their drinks from the bar, Lorenzo began to introduce Yvonne to his friends who were pleasant, friendly and seemed very accepting of her. As Lorenzo turned away to speak to a man in his twenties, a tall, fit-looking and well-dressed young woman in her late twenties with long blond hair sidled up to Yvonne.

"Is he talking to Jay again?"

"I'm sorry, I don't know his name," responded Yvonne politely. She glanced at the woman next to her sipping a martini.

"I don't think I know your name either. I'm Yvonne." She held out her hand as part of the introduction.

"I'm Charlie. Well, Charlene actually, but everyone calls me Charlie." She accepted Yvonne's outstretched hand.

"Pleased to meet you, Charlie. So, how do you know Lorenzo?"

"God, who doesn't know Lorenzo. I swear he trains everyone who's someone. He used to be my trainer," sighed Charlie wistfully.

"Do I detect a little bit of 'oh I fancy him' in there?" Yvonne, laughed happy in the knowledge that she was in the company of a man that so many women wanted. This was like Gillian all over again. Yvonne realised that any form of jealousy could endanger her relationship with Lorenzo, besides it was never in her nature to be clingy or possessive. As long as she felt loved and that she was the sole recipient of that love she was secure. She was brought back to the present by Charlie's animated response.

"Jesus, you'd need to be a nun not to fancy him, but don't tell my man," she joked. She attempted to nudge Yvonne playfully at her remark, but she stumbled and spilt some of her drink across a table. She erupted into a fit of giggles, while Yvonne looked on disdainful, public drunkenness was so not her style.

"I tell you what though, he never mixes business and pleasure, it's his golden rule." Charlie took a big sip of her drink, which was now almost empty. "I'll tell you a little secret." Charlie continued as she leaned closer, "he's shocked everyone coming here with you tonight. He's rarely seen with a female friend."

"Meaning exactly what?"

Charlie threw her hands up to show that she had not meant any offence. "I didn't mean that he's gay or anything like that. Just that he's more secluded than your average lad…"

She didn't have a chance to finish her thought because Lorenzo strolled over to the table with two snifter glasses sparkling with amber liquid.

"So, what are you ladies talking about?" grinned Lorenzo, as he created space for himself at the table. He placed one brandy on the table in front of Yvonne and winked suggestively.

"We were just, um…" Charlie was struggling to explain, the blush across her face only just visible in the low club light.

"We were talking about girly things." Yvonne interrupted to save the conversation and Charlie from any further embarrassment.

"What were you and Jay talking about?" inquired Charlie, quickly recovering.

"Oh, you know, boy things," he mocked, laughing at his reinterpretation of her answer

"Lorenzo, you are a dark horse, keeping silent about this lovely lady."

Yvonne could see that Charlie liked to know everything about everything and would not stop until she had the full story.

"Well, Charlie, I had to because if I told you, then everyone on earth would know."

"Aw, thanks, Lorenzo," she replied, batting her eyelashes flirtatiously. "So, I take it you know everything about this guy, Yvonne?"

"All that I need to know, thank you."

"Well, you've got a cracker there. He's so ultra-fussy about his ladies, that's why we hardly ever see him with anyone," she went on, "so count yourself a lucky lady."

"Oh, I do." Yvonne looped her arm around Lorenzo's waist and rested her head on his shoulder. *I do feel a lucky lady, and he makes it apparent he feels like a lucky man,* she thought to herself.

He kissed the top of her head before excusing himself as there was someone by the bar who motioned to speak to him.

"This seems a friendly crowd of people," Yvonne remarked to Charlie as he walked away.

"Yeah, this is the premier league of Glasgow, all very well-off and successful."

"I suppose Lorenzo is the personal trainer to all of them, then it would explain how he knows so many people." Yvonne continued to survey the room, as Lorenzo made a round of yet more of the crowd.

"Oh, hell yeah all of them, most have their own companies. Dave there is a lawyer, Grant is a doctor, and me, well I'm a writer and storyteller. What about you, Yvonne?"

This was a startling revelation. Yvonne never passed up an opportunity to network or take on more clients, even if they were annoying women who panted over her boyfriend.

"I have my own publishing company. Do you have a publisher for your work, Charlie?"

"Not at the moment, I just self-publish."

"Well if I can help you in any way, please don't hesitate to contact me."

Yvonne pulled out a business card from her small bag and handed it to Charlie, wondering if it would be lost the next minute. She shrugged her shoulders, that was what prospects were, the possibility.

"Thanks, I will do that. You know, I'm pleased for Lorenzo, he needs a woman in his life. He's been alone too long." At that, Yvonne felt an arm slipping around her waist and pulling her in gently, discreetly signalling that it was time to leave.

"Shall we slip away quietly? You have work tomorrow," he whispered in her ear. Even though they were so close, she still had to strain to hear him over the music.

"Yes, I would love to." She smiled and squeezed his hand.

"I hope to see you again, Yvonne," said Charlie who leaned in for a hug, struggling to keep her balance.

"Oh, I'm sure you will." Yvonne reluctantly let herself be embraced.

Charlie watched Lorenzo take Yvonne's hand as he led her from the club and out onto Albion Street then turned to order another martini.

"Okay, you have a couple of options, Miss Duncan, either join the queue and wait for a taxi home or come back with me for a nightcap?"

Yvonne viewed the long line of taxis and the clamouring queues that were quickly becoming pushy, as taxi rank stewards struggled to keep order.

"Mmmm, that is a difficult choice, but may I settle for a nightcap?" She was happy to extend her night and time with Lorenzo.

"Good choice, I hate standing in a queue." He looked delighted with her answer.

"My pet hate," she agreed, as she slipped her hand into his.

They meandered along the road and watched others making their way home – some couples hand-in-hand, while others were not so harmonious. One couple was using the open air to shout obscenities at each other, doubting their legitimacy and airing misdemeanours from the past, while someone else unloaded her evening's drink into the gutter next to them, before staggering in the direction of a taxi which was unlikely to take her anywhere.

When Lorenzo closed the door to his apartment, it was as if the world was shut out. No drunks or unhappy couples, just the two of them in their perfect little bubble.

"Brandy?"

"Yes please."

He lifted a crystal decanter from the small bar in a corner of the living room. Two matching crystal glasses received a generous amount of fine amber liquid. Lorenzo handed a glass to Yvonne before sitting next to her on the luxurious and comfortable settee. He lifted a sleek handset from a small table next to him, which resulted in the room lights slowly dimming as relaxing music began to play subtly from the speakers.

Yvonne turned her body side-on and curled her legs beneath her, her head on the cushion behind her, all the while the glass of brandy held securely in her left hand. She felt so relaxed as she looked at Lorenzo. His head rested on the cushion behind him and his eyes were closed as he listened to the music. She let her eyes wander down from his jaw, stopping at the hollow of his neck which was exposed when he loosened his tie earlier in the evening.

"What is going on in that curious mind of yours?" he inquired gently, as if fully aware that Yvonne was observing him. He opened one eye lazily to contemplate as she answered.

"I'm wondering why someone like you is with someone like me, tonight?"

"What does that mean?" he asked, furrowing his brow

"We went into Arthur's and there was hardly anyone in there that didn't know you."

"I know a lot of people, a lot of people know me." He reached out to put his hand on her thigh and closed his eyes again.

"What I can tell you is that a lot of my friends were seriously attracted to you."

"And your response was?"

"I told them that you were out of bounds." He replied as he brought up her hand to his lips and gently brushed it with a soft kiss.

She could feel a blush spreading across her cheeks again – how can he do this so easily to me? She rested her head on his shoulder and let out a small almost inaudible sigh.

"I hate to end this evening, but I do have work in the morning."

"Oh sorry, shall I get you a taxi or do you want to use the guest room?"

"Tell you what…" she ventured.

"What?" He sat up, interested.

"Give me three reasons why I need a taxi?"

His eyes sparkled with amusement. "One, you need to get home. Two, you have work in the morning. Three… I can't think of a third."

"Failed," she giggled, cuddling into him. "Now give me three reasons why I should be in the guest room."

"Oh, that's easy. One, you're my guest. Two, you have work tomorrow. Three, you have to make breakfast," he listed quickly as he began kissing her neck.

"No, the last one doesn't count," she laughed, not wanting his affection to stop, but not wanting to be too easy either.

"Oh, I give up, this is a daft game," and he pulled her in closer until she was on his lap.

His face had moved down from her neck to explore her, tickle her collarbone, and continue to feather kisses lower.

"Bed then?" She wrapped her legs around him and lifted his face to kiss him passionately.

"Good idea, Miss Duncan," he agreed, lifting her with him as he stood up. "Listen, before we go have you ever been to Sardinia?" he asked.

"No."

"Good," he said, striding towards the bedroom, holding Yvonne up as her legs stayed wrapped around his waist.

Chapter Six

As the alarm sounded at seven o'clock, Yvonne stirred. She felt a bit groggy, having had little sleep. She moved slowly, her naked body resting against his, she tried not to disturb him until she felt his arm pull her closer and he hugged her tight.

"Where are you sneaking off to?" He whispered into her hair.

"Some of us have to go to work," she whispered back. "Also, I now have to go home and get changed first."

"Please stay," he looked up at her imploringly, his eyes pleading.

"Lorenzo, behave," she giggled as she shoved him playfully away.

"Yeah, okay," he huffed. "The keys for the Range Rover are on the table. Take that if you have a licence."

"Are you kidding me?" she gawked.

"Not at all. I am not getting up to take you home," he said defiantly, cuddling into her. She enjoyed the feeling of his arms wrapped around her. "Yvonne?"

"What?" she sighed, only slightly miffed that she was having to get herself home. He looked too cute in the morning with his fluffy hair and bleary eyes to be really upset with him

"Thank you for last night, and for being you," he said as he kissed her shoulder.

She leaned over and kissed him gently on his forehead and then on his lips. She studied him lying there, noting every detail about him.

"Hey you, don't be late, or I'll tell the boss."

"I am the boss," she retaliated as she watched him turn over. "Lorenzo, may I take the Ferrari instead?"

"Sure, if you ever become Mrs Maldini and not before. Now go away." He had buried his face into the pillow and his voice was muffled, which was her cue to leave.

She laughed softly.

"See you later," she purred against his skin as she tickled his shoulder with her tongue.

"Good morning all." Yvonne voiced her usual greeting as strode smiling into the office her business persona firmly intact.

Although she recognised that she felt a vitalisation from her vigorous evening, she did not realise that it also left her with a happy and contended glow. The staff glanced at each other, unsure what to make of this new chirpier demeanour. This was still Yvonne, the boss, but not as they had ever seen her before.

As she waltzed through the office, a question was fired in her direction by her longest-serving employee, Gordon Holmes. "Yvonne, were you in Arthur's last night?"

The pointed comment, delivered in an off-hand way, caused her to briefly pause in her steps and without missing a beat, she affirmed, "Yes, I was actually."

She then stopped and waited for him to acknowledge her answer, quietly interested in where this conversation was going to go.

"You seemed to be in some… salubrious company."

"Meaning what, Gordon?" She turned to see him grinning from his desk.

"Well… oh wait a minute." He rose from his chair and looked down onto the car park below. "Range Rover, Yvonne? You don't normally drive in the city."

"It belongs to a friend."

"Must be some friend arriving in that at nine o'clock in the morning." Gordon muttered and focused in on the number plate that read 2 LM. He knew exactly who that car belonged to and it did not take a rocket scientist to work out what Yvonne had been up to. It was just such a deviation from her reserved personal life.

"Right, that's enough supposition if you like working here, Gordon," she chided, laughing to curb the severity of her remark.

He made an offhand comment about a clapped-out Toyota that she was welcome to use, which she chose to ignore as she resumed her journey to her office.

Closing the door behind her, Yvonne picked up her mobile and dialled.

"Good morning again." The smile she was wearing shone through her tone.

"Good morning, again to you too," responded the seductive, sleepy voice.

"So… Sardinia. Were you serious?"

"What do *you* think?" His plain tone left no doubt as to the sincerity of his intentions for their trip.

The attention that he paid to her left her nothing short of giddy.

"Lorenzo, I don't know day from night when I'm with you and more importantly, I don't care."

"Yes, I was perfectly serious. I want you to come with me so I can introduce you to my family, most of which is in Sardinia."

She heard how gentle his tone was and she knew he was smiling. The thought of his smile set off a million butterflies in her stomach. "Well, I've checked my passport and I'm good for travel."

"Is that a yes then?"

Before she could confirm, their conversation was interrupted by Yvonne's receptionist knocking on the door. "Yvonne, Anne on the phone for you."

"Lorenzo, I have to go, there's an urgent call for the boss," she explained hurriedly before she hung up.

Yvonne picked up her office receiver, softening her tone. "Hi, Anne. How are you?"

"Yvonne, the police have recovered a body from Loch Lomond and they want me to see if it is my dad, but from the description, it's almost definitely him they say." Yvonne knew Anne had been crying by the breathy hiccups that were coming down the phone. There was a brief pause then after a shaky breath she continued, "you know, in one way, I hope it's my dad, and in another way, I hope it's not."

"I know what you mean, just remember that we are here for you, and Anne, keep in touch."

Yvonne heard the click of a receiver as it disconnected, then put the phone down herself.

The elation of being with Lorenzo drained quickly after the emotional telephone call with Anne. Her head hung heavily in her hands as she leaned over her desk. Taking a deep breath, she composed herself before leaving her office to announce, "Team meeting please!"

She scanned the conference room as her team gathered around her, pens ready to scribble instructions on the notepads in front of them.

"Right guys, where are we at? Gordon, you first."

"I have two books still in the editing stage, one is due back to the author and the other is in formatting, both still on schedule. There are a few questions that have been fired back to the newest author for clarification on the changes they want to make to our contract."

Yvonne raised her eyebrows.

"No boss nothing to do with the royalty just a few marketing requirements. It's all under control."

Yvonne nodded approvingly. She asked the same of Janine, Amy and Sam who comprised the rest of her small company. They all had similarly satisfactory replies as each answered going around the table following the usual meeting style dictated by Yvonne's compulsive organisational requirements.

"I have a few on the go as well but trying to get the authors to reply is a nightmare." Janine rolled her eyes.

"All good with me, authors and illustrators working in unison so we're on target. I just need approval on a few of the new marketing plans." Amy shuffled the artwork in order of priority.

"We have about a dozen new authors lined up for the backlist. Quality is good and definitely be enough to keep us ticking over without having to add new staff." Sam was always diligent in her efforts to keep the company on a strict budget.

Yvonne was reassured that her business had enough ongoing and upcoming projects to keep the company not only alive but thriving. Now it was time to share the delicate news about Anne's father. Taking a deep breath, she steeled her nerves to deliver the delicate news.

"Right, that's all great and thank you for those updates. Now I have some information for you. Anne called to say that a body has been recovered from Loch Lomond." Yvonne continued before the startled responses interrupted. "The police believe that it is her father and so she has to go and make an official identification. She believes that it's her dad, so if any of you get a call from her, please be careful what you say."

After the nods of assent Yvonne finished the meeting. "Okay, back to desks folks, these books won't publish themselves."

Later that morning her mobile buzzed. "Hey you," she answered seeing Lorenzo's name on the screen.

"Hey babe, do you want to keep a hold of 2 LM?"

"No, I want to get on a bus and a train," she pleaded. "I just want to be me like I was before you came along." She rolled her eyes, knowing that he'd be able to picture it. "Why are you asking?"

"Well, I was searching around the internet and I found a set of plates, YDP 1, that we could get put onto the Range Rover."

She was stunned into silence as she worked out what those initials meant.

"Yvonne Duncan Publications 1," he spelt out for her, unsure what was taking her so long to reply.

"I got it Lorenzo. But I can't let you do that!"

"Too late. They arrive tomorrow."

"I don't have a car to put them on," she argued.

"Yes, you do. I just said we'll put them on the Range Rover. I can go get a little run-around today for myself and put the 2 LM plates on that."

"Lorenzo, what do you mean by a 'little run-around?" Yvonne could feel her voice straining as she struggled to comprehend the magnitude of what he was offering her, and feeling her independent nature rebel. She had never met anyone so generous.

"Just a basic car to help with the day-to-day errands. Don't worry about it."

Just as she had earlier, Yvonne's receptionist appeared at the door, gesturing at the office phone urgently. Yvonne nodded in acknowledgement, before teasing Lorenzo down the phone, "Go away, I have work to do." They exchanged swift goodbyes as she clicked onto her office line.

"H-, hi Yvonne," sobbed Anne from the other end of the line. "It is my dad. Yvonne. My dad is... he's really dead!" An explosion of tears interrupted.

After a few moments Yvonne heard snuffles and blowing of a nose before Anne continued. "They're going to do a post-mortem later today. I'll get back to you soon."

"Please do, and give my condolences to your family. I am so, so, sorry. Don't forget I'm here if you need anything at all and take as much time off as you need."

There was a knock at her door from Gordon, and she waved him in.

"You okay?" he asked tentatively, sensing the aura of despair hovering around her.

"No, not really. It was Anne's father they recovered from the Loch."

"Geez... that is sad," he ventured in an attempt at solidarity confirmation.

"Sorry, Gordon. What was it you wanted?" she asked shaking herself back to the present.

Over the next few minutes, they discussed further details from the meeting, authors who were currently on the books and others who were being considered for distribution. Gordon sensed that her mind was elsewhere and decided to take advantage of her rare vulnerability as he knew never to probe into his boss's personal life.

"Yvonne, I have to ask you something, and it is because I care about you, you do know that everyone cares about you."

"Okay… is this something to do with Arthur's by chance?"

"No, it's nothing to do with the place, but rather the company you were in."

"Right. If you must know, I was with Lorenzo Maldini, who is a friend of mine. The others I've never met before in my life," she replied sternly, almost defensively, chastising him for quizzing her about her private life.

A relieved smile broke out across Gordon's face, the tension melting from his shoulder.

"Listen, Yvonne, Lorenzo is well-known, he's a cracking guy and successful, but some of the others… just be careful, please."

Yvonne had not missed the comment about Lorenzo and concluded that Gordon would be able to fill in some gaps for her. "Gordon, please tell me everything you know about Lorenzo."

"Why just him?"

"Just answer my question!" Swiftly shutting down his line of questioning.

"Yvonne, in all the years I've known you, you've always got a train or bus into work, yet this morning I see you arriving in a Range Rover with one of Lorenzo's personal plates on it."

Yvonne raised her eyebrows as she waited for him to go on, wondering how he knew that.

"Everyone knows that he lives in one of the most luxurious apartments in Merchant City and has extravagant tastes. He's young and very wary of anyone attempting to get into his private life, which makes sense. Before you arrived with him last night, nobody had ever seen him looking so comfortable in the company of a woman. He's a really shy person but one hell of a businessman."

He took a breath, summoning the courage to ask for a piece of personal information from his boss. "Can I ask you? How you met him?"

"He's my personal trainer. So how is it you know so much about him?" Her tone was guarded, unwilling to give too much away while trying to find out as much as she could.

"You know he probably owns the gym you train at, right?" quizzed Gordon, continuing his subdued assessment of the situation.

Yvonne's head shot up at that revelation. "What do you mean?"

"He owns gyms all over the place, literally the length and breadth of Scotland, and he's quickly moving into the North of England. He's like Midas, everything he touches turns to gold. He buys failing businesses, makes them successful and sells them on. You must be the only woman in Glasgow that doesn't know about him."

She took a moment to process this before asking her next question. "Where is he from?"

"Somewhere in Italy. We all joke that he's linked to the Mafia."

"Thank you Gordon." Yvonne's tone was dismissive yet not unfriendly.

He stood up to leave. "No problem Yvonne. Just be careful that he's not sniffing around here to buy this."

"Thanks for that also, but as we've just established, this business is anything but failing," she quipped sarcastically, watching him leave her office.

She leaned back in her substantial and comfortable black leather chair, pondering what Gordon had just revealed about Lorenzo and his success. She picked up her mobile phone and with a few taps was soon staring at Lorenzo's private number. He had emphasised how few people had access to this particular number, and wondered if there was some deeper meaning to that in light of this new information, something more dubious. Yvonne sat staring at the screen completely conflicted. She knew she was falling in love and adored him and the feeling, however those long-term trust issues were raising a red flag. Her business had been her life for almost twenty years. She wanted to trust him but she also knew that she had to find out if he was planning a takeover. Fuelled by an instinctive possessiveness of the company that she had built from the ground up, she dialled the number on the screen.

"I was just thinking about you," he drawled seductively as he answered the phone.

"What were you thinking?"

"If I can take you out for lunch? I can't wait to see you again."

That looming feeling she'd experienced earlier when he had offered her the car was creeping back. "Lorenzo, we have to talk."

"What about?"

"Us... if there is an us."

His tone suddenly turned urgent as he implored, "Yvonne, please leave the office and get back here. Now."

"Okay, I'll see you in about half an hour," she conceded. Hanging up the phone, she carefully got her bag together. The Range Rover keys were heavy in her hand. As she stepped out, she spoke clearly across the office to ensure everyone heard her. "Guys, I have a meeting with a new author. I'll be back later, but I have my mobile if anyone needs me in the meantime."

"Sure, no problem, boss," acknowledged Gordon with a knowing glint in his eye.

As she drove carefully towards Lorenzo's flat, the roads clear of any traffic, Yvonne could not help wondering if she was being set up. The only way to find out was to meet the situation head-on, which she fully intended to do. She had not worked so long, so hard and devoted so much of her life to create one of the most successful indie publishing houses in Scotland, only to have someone to snatch it away from her. This brought up all the issues with trust, trusting people had only led to heartbreak and she would not allow this to happen again, so she let her anger fuel her as she waited for the main door to open, before storming up to his flat.

"Right, you! Sit down!" Slamming the keys of the Range Rover into Lorenzo's hand Yvonne continued her tirade. "Do you know who you're messing with?"

Her ferocity shocked and confused him. "What's wrong, Yvonne?"

"You, me, it's over! I regret staying here last night, and as for Sardinia, you can forget that! Oh, and another thing! My business is not for sale!"

Her chest was heaving with indignant rage, her nostrils flared and her stance over him was intimidating. "And see your Mafia pals? They haven't met me yet," she threatened, jabbing her finger into his chest. Her face had turned almost the same shade of red as her hair, and her temper was just as fiery.

"Yvonne," he coaxed soothingly, trying to balance out her increasingly manic energy. "Please sit down."

"Why should I?" Her voice deepened into a more menacing tone.

"Because I'm asking you to," his voice responded in a gentle, soft and soothing manner.

"This had better be good," she muttered, breathing heavily. Her piercing gaze was frosty as he pulled her down slowly next to him.

"Where did all this come from?" His tone still calm, creating just enough space between them and allowing her to cool down.

"All what?" Her arms were crossed defensively across her chest.

"All this crap about the Mafia, buying your business, all that."

She looked him straight in the eye. "I've just been told about you – the gyms, buying failing businesses, all of it. Is that really what you do? Is that how you afford all those cars? And this place?" gesturing around to prove her point.

She was beginning to settle and carefully observed the change in his facial expression and his body language as he folded his arms, shutting himself off.

"I don't know who you've been speaking to, but they know nothing about me or my family."

"Lorenzo, talk to me now or I swear I am gone forever."

He paused, weighing up how to broach the subject. "Right, the gyms. My family has gyms across Scotland. I only manage them, but everyone thinks I own them."

"Go on."

"I do own 2 LM, so you had my car today."

She interrupted him before he could continue. "And what about LM 1?"

"That belongs to my father, Leonardo Maldini. I do have access to that car, so everyone thinks I own that as well, which is definitely not the case and why I didn't want you to drive it this morning."

She nodded, it seemed to be a reasonable and satisfactory explanation about the cars, but she was not quite ready to let go though. There was still the most important point to clear up.

"And buying businesses?"

"Again, my father. He's the king of turning businesses around. I'm his apprentice, nothing more."

He had laid his hands across his knees, palms up, prompting a calm discussion in place of the rowdy argument.

"That still means that you're learning how to turn businesses for your own profit. What about my business?" Her tone serious although receptive to his honesty. "Do you want that?"

"No, just the owner," he answered smoothly, as he tried his luck at pulling her in closer. She resisted, needing a final piece of affirmation.

"I'm going to ask you something and if you are lying to me, I swear I will cut your balls off, do you understand?"

"Yes," he replied solemnly.

"Why are you sitting here in your dressing gown when it's almost midday?" she teased, with a hint of a smile as she finally let herself relax.

"My first appointment isn't until three o'clock. If you had stayed here this morning, then you would've known that and none of this would ever have happened."

This time, she did not resist as he pulled her onto his lap and kissed the tip of her nose.

"I'm sorry," she conceded, finally calming down. "It's just… I've known you for such a short time and I'm…I'm… just mad about you! But I also love my business, and I had to make sure that it was, is, and will remain safe. Trusting people is something that I do not do easily."

"I'm not just people, am I?"

Lorenzo felt a small shake of her head against his chest and pulled Yvonne more tightly into his embrace.

"Now, what about Sardinia?" he asked quietly.

She remained silent as she considered the invite. All her energy had left her after her outburst. With a deep sigh, she accepted his offer. "Lorenzo, I am sorry for that outburst and it's a yes to Sardinia for a holiday and to meet your family, but the promise to cut your balls off if you mess with me remains in place."

Finishing that statement she gave him a large exaggerated wink.

He beamed, nuzzling into her neck in celebration. "Yvonne Duncan, we are heading for Sardinia." He paused in thought for a few seconds before following up with, "oh, and I have to get you a security card to get you in here."

Chapter Seven

"You do realise if I don't get up and get back to work, I'll never make my first million, far less my second and you have an appointment with a client soon."

Lorenzo made no reply as she stood up gracefully from the bed, simply watching Yvonne walk around his bedroom naked, picking her clothes off the floor methodically. She paused in her tracks, acutely aware of his eyes on her.

"And what are you looking at Mr. Maldini?"

"You. You're just... so beautiful. Yvonne, this has never happened to me before. Being like... this, and the feelings I have for you," he stammered as he lay on his side, resting his head on his hand. His usual smooth and confident exterior had cracked, revealing a shy young man. It made him all the more endearing.

She walked over to him, leaned over and kissed his lips gently, "Maybe you're just infatuated with the older woman, you devil."

"Only you," he teased in earnest as he watched her getting dressed.

"How did the interview go, Yvonne?" inquired Gordon as she breezed into the office working hard not to show all the symptoms of a lovesick schoolgirl.

"Great. Fabulous in fact," she acknowledged, placing her briefcase on her desk. "Anyone for coffee?"

There was a flurry of concerned glances, none of which were picked up on by Yvonne who was lost in an ongoing daydream of Lorenzo. None of her employees could work out what was going on with their boss. First, asking to join them at the pub, then going out on the town, and now volunteering herself for a coffee run? It was all too much for any one of them to work out.

"Are you okay, Yvonne?" asked Amy carefully, expressing the concern that they were all feeling.

Yvonne was startled from her romantic reverie. "Yes, why would I not be okay?"

"It's just that you've been acting differently for the past few days. You are... radiant," Amy stammered, struggling to find the correct adjective to describe Yvonne's current state.

"Maybe she's in love," joked Gordon.

"Gordon, you know me better than that. My only love is this business."

"Yeah, yeah, Yvonne, you're all work and no play," he mocked, looking at her with a wry smile.

"Right, you can get your own coffee now. I have work to get on with."

Closing her office door firmly behind her, she sat down behind her desk to call Lorenzo, but he beat her to it, almost as if he had read her mind from afar.

"Hiya, I was just about to call you," purred Yvonne.

"Do you know what you've done? You've stolen my Range Rover," he teased. "That means you have to pick me up after work tonight."

She could not help beaming at the thought of another night with Lorenzo. "What time?"

"Ten."

"Okay."

I must get a grip of myself, she thought. Giddy after their conversation she knew that back to work was a priority, however, as she stared out into the office at her staff, she had only one thing on her mind, and it had everything to do with Lorenzo.

Finally it truly dawned on her, *I've worked hard all my life, I deserve this love. Yes you do said her other half - but will I allow you to have it?*

A few hours later Yvonne turned her monitor off right on time. She packed her bag and stepped out of her office.

"Right guys, five o'clock. You're all on your own time now. See you tomorrow. Gordon, have you got a minute please before I go?"

"Yeah, I've always got a minute for you, Yvonne. Is it about the new author?"

"Indeed."

As Gordon sat down, Yvonne closed her office door at his back. "Gordon, I appreciate what you told me today, and I acknowledge that you were acting in my best interest."

He nodded waiting to find out what it was she literally wanted to say. She rushed the rest of her speech speaking confidently. "I went out and interviewed the new author and we've ironed everything out and I now know what he's all about. Sadly, there are a lot of rumours and suppositions about him, just because he keeps himself to himself, just like someone else you know. Anyway, these are all false, so I am not going to expand on anything, but I just want to say thanks for looking out for me."

"They say that love is blind, Yvonne, please just take care."

Gordon closed the door on the way out just as her office phone rang. She sighed, desperate to get home and freshen up before seeing Lorenzo later, however, professionalism dictated she take the call.

"Yvonne? It's Anne again. I'm not going to be back at work for a few weeks. I have a lot to take care of for my mum."

"That's completely understandable, as I said earlier take all the time you need. You have nothing to worry about here. I want to reassure you that your job here is safe and I'll pay your full salary for the next four weeks, and then we will see where we go from there, okay?"

"Oh, Yvonne, you don't have to do that."

There was a lull in the conversation and Yvonne could tell that Anne was working up the nerve to say something else. "We received the post-mortem results today."

"Oh?" was the only response Yvonne could muster.

"Dad died of a massive heart attack and that caused him to fall into the water. They said he was dead before he went in."

Yvonne could not stop the gasp that escaped from her lips. Her shoulders slumped as a wave of relief washed over her.

"Oh, Anne, I am so sorry."

"I'll let you know when we'll have the funeral."

"Yes, please do. See you then." Yvonne placed the phone in the receiver, and she slumped back into her chair, while the relief that flooded through her body almost drained her completely of energy. All she was waiting on now was the conclusion of the investigation at Grove Park. She could do without the police tracking her back to that location.

Yvonne drove home and parked the Range Rover near her flat. Walking into Asraf's shop, she lifted a few groceries and took them to the counter. As she moved through the aisles, she caught sight of her stranger at the counter and overheard a slight New York drawl as he spoke to Asraf. She had never heard him speak before and was surprised by the accent.

"Miss Duncan," whispered Asraf, a panicked look in his eyes as he scanned around his little shop, "who is the big American guy that comes in here?"

"I don't have a clue Asraf. I've seen him around, but I don't know who he is. Why do you ask?"

"It just seems that every time you are in here, he is not far away," Asraf continued in his urgent and concerned whisper.

She took her shopping bag and bestowed one of her most endearing smiles on him. "Thank you, Asraf, but there is nothing to worry about. See you soon."

Yvonne hurried across the road and took the steps two at a time to her flat. Once she had placed her briefcase on the floor as normal, she went through her routine of checking each of the rooms. Years ago, her flat had been broken into and she had disturbed the raiders by coming home earlier than anticipated.

Now, she experienced the same physiological response every time she entered her empty flat; that fear that someone would be there waiting for her. She could not help her racing heartbeat and uncontrollable shaking. Her palms would remain clammy until she was certain each room was as empty as it should be. It all came back to trust, trusting that her home was her safe haven. She shook her head to dislodge the memory and bring herself back into the present moment. After completing her ritualistic walkthrough, it was evident that all was well and everything was where it should be.

As she walked over to the large bay window of the living room, she saw the American stranger strolling into his close. She waited impatiently for him to appear in his flat. Having been so wrapped up in Lorenzo recently, she had not seen him for a while. The realisation caused the smallest squirm of anxiety in the pit of her stomach. Would he take up his usual position where he could see her clearly? She fervently hoped he would.

Circumstances had changed dramatically since their last encounter. Lorenzo was in her life now. Was she prepared to destroy what she had with him, just for the thrill that coursed through her body when she saw her stranger?

Then again, he also seemed to have a girlfriend, or at least a female in his life, as she had recently seen. She watched intently as he walked between the living room and the kitchen, and back again. He eventually stopped and stood in the middle of the living room, looking over at her place.

She could feel the tension rising and she knew that something exhilarating was about to happen. This secret that she and the unknown neighbour had together excited her. *Will he make the first move*, she wondered as she put on the small light in the living room. He did the same, illuminating his living room.

What harm were they really doing? It is not as if he had seen her naked, as Lorenzo had. Neither had she seen him naked. Her heart was racing in anticipation. This was just a game, a little bit of harmless fun.

Her neighbour with the New York drawl was the first to make a move as he slowly stripped off his clothes. His white shirt and his jeans fell to the floor to reveal his usual tight underwear. He folded his arms as if defiantly signalling to her that it was her turn, or else he would stop playing.

She stared intensely across the road as she stripped off her jacket and blouse, before removing her trousers, leaving her in her scarlet silk bra and matching thong. She slightly lacked her usual graceful finesse hurrying, anxious to see what his next move would be. Instead of turning around as he normally would, he dropped the last of the clothing while staring directly at her. Her first time seeing him naked. Her breathing was heavy and rapid. Her heart was pounding with unencumbered excitement. Nothing was hidden from her as she had a clear view of his body, from his chiselled abs, all the way down, and it was obvious that he wanted her. *What am I doing!* She screamed at herself internally as she slipped off her bra before turning to face him, she then slipped her finger along the band to drop her thong and exposing her body to him for the first time. The sexual tension was coursing through her veins as he turned and walked away. She did likewise. Heading to her bedroom she pulled on casual clothes not really trying to regain composure, as she wanted to bottle up this thrill for Lorenzo, later.

At ten o'clock precisely, she was at the gym in the Range Rover to pick up Lorenzo. As he left the building, she flung herself towards him, wrapping her arms around his neck. She kissed him deeply and passionately, unable to get close enough to him.

He pulled away first. "Wow. What did I do to deserve that?"

"Not calling the police to say I had stolen your car," she giggled.

"Oh, I have other plans to make you pay for that," he growled against her neck, making her giggle even more.

"Really?"

"Yes, really."

"Your place or mine?" she asked, practically panting with unbridled lust.

"You drive to wherever you want."

"Okay," she replied, "mine is closer."

I wonder if he'll see us.

Closing the door behind them, she spun him around and before he knew what was happening, she was pressed against him, kissing him intensely, while her hands scrambled to remove his tracksuit top. Lorenzo wasted no time in removing her clothing either, and they clung to each other, stumbling through the apartment, crashing onto her bed.

Later they both lay there, fulfilled and exhausted, he looked at the clock on the bedside table, easy to see from the moonlight slicing through the room. It read one-thirty.

"Yvonne?" Lorenzo ventured tentatively into the darkness.

"Uh-huh?"

"That was amazing. If that's what stealing my car does to you, steal it again. Please?"

She responded by giving him a playful slap on the arm. Saying nothing, lying on her side she cuddled into his body. She draped her leg over him, and he wrapped himself around her, each ensuring that the other was going nowhere soon.

"Look what you've done to me, Lorenzo Maldini. I'm a soppy wreck because of you," she whispered.

"I can't get you out of my head, Yvonne." He paused then whispered back, "I'm not perfect. I have my faults like everyone, but if there is one certain thing, it's that I will be faithful to you as long as we are together."

They both drifted off to sleep, each content in their lover's embrace.

At seven in the morning, the alarm sounded and Yvonne groggily rose from her bed to put on the kettle for morning coffee, before stepping into the shower. A few minutes later, she went back into the bedroom wrapped in a large white fluffy towel and he sat on the bed with her back to Lorenzo who appeared to be sleeping. As she dried herself off, she suddenly felt light, tender kisses making their way up her shoulder and her neck, sending tingles up and down the length of her spine.

"That better be Mr Maldini doing this to me," she breathed seductively.

"Uh-huh," was the muffled reply as he wrapped his hand in her hair.

"I have work to go to," she pleaded, her resolve weakening.

"You told me you owned the business, which means you can be a little late." He flipped her onto her back and pulled her towards him.

"I'm never late Lorenzo, behave."

He did not. Instead, he started kissing her neck and making his way down the valley between her breasts, then her stomach… she half-heartedly pleaded with him to stop.

"I said…" as she moaned, "oh hell, Lorenzo, is this what life is like with a younger man? You have so much energy."

"I am trying to keep up with all of your energy." He grinned as he continued kissing her all over.

After another hour together in bed, Yvonne lay on her front, propping herself upwards with her arms folded under her.

As he lay on his back looking up at her he explained, "While it is a holiday, the main reason I'm taking you to Sardinia is to meet my family."

"And when is that going to happen?"

"We can fly out on Friday night at seven-thirty and back in on Monday. Think of it has a long weekend, I know you wouldn't want to be away from the office for a week."

"God, you are good." She ran her hand through his hair, appreciating his consistent thoughtfulness.

"So, is that okay with you?"

"It has to be I suppose, although it is definitely going to cause chaos with the office gossips." She giggled, and then she kissed him. "Right, get up, get dressed, you are coming with me. Mr Maldini, new author of keep-fit books and my newest client, we have a meeting."

"Eh?" He looked confused.

"Just do as you're told."

The office clock glared nine o'clock at the office staff. No morning greeting from Yvonne, no morning meeting update, no Yvonne, for the first time ever workaholic Yvonne Duncan was going to be late. Yet another out-of-character development for her business persona.

Chapter Eight

Lorenzo drove them both to Yvonne's office and pulled into the private car park. She led the way, calling the lift to take them to the floor that housed Yvonne Duncan Publications. She was nervous about facing her staff, over an hour and a half late for the first time since she started the company.

Taking a deep breath, she pulled open the office door with the normal greeting.

"Good morning, all," and before anyone had a chance to question her she plunged ahead. "Let me introduce to you Lorenzo Maldini, one of Scotland's top fitness coaches. Even though he has a degree in English Literature, he has never written a book in his life. Now we are going to change all that, with a health and fitness book."

A cacophony of female voices erupted, clamouring to help with the project. Gordon just looked on sardonically from his desk.

"Ladies, please put your tongues back into your heads and stop drooling over your desks. Gordon, would you please take this one?"

Looking around he quipped, "I'm sure one of the girls would like to take this one."

Yvonne glared at him. "I'm sure all of the girls would like to take this one, but you are the most experienced, which is why I want you to take the job. You are actually quite good at what you do, you know that? So, you will provide the right guidance to Lorenzo as a debut author."

"Tea or coffee, Mr Maldini?" chirped Amy, sidling up behind them.

"Neither, thank you. I had some before I left the house this morning."

"Was that a drink or something else?" she asked wickedly.

"Both."

This simple, strong answer left Amy with a searing blush across her cheeks. In her mid-twenties, slim, about five feet three inches tall in heels and straight brown hair which touched her waist, she was in her usual attire of jeans designer, t-shirt and jacket. Lorenzo gave her a quick wink causing her to blush even further.

"Amy, don't you have some work to do?" Yvonne queried from her office.

Amy dashed back to her desk as Lorenzo walked into Yvonne's office and sat down facing her, crossing his legs. He surveyed the minimalistic, modern office. "You're even more attractive when you go into boss mode. I'm impressed."

"With what?"

"You're already all over this project, I can see that. I wish I could build a business like yours from the ground up just as you have."

Yvonne paused, her eyes narrowing as she looked up from her computer.

"Well you have the businesses that you buy, fix, and run. You don't need mine." Yvonne's eyes flashed.

Lorenzo tried to perceive by the tone of her voice if she was getting annoyed, or if she wanted a further explanation. He had not meant anything but to compliment her and also knew that it was important for her to understand that he was only interested in her, not her business. He rubbed his face with both hands before sitting back in his chair, creating some space between the two of them.

"Listen, Yvonne, I honestly did not mean anything by that, I really do admire you. Your business savvy, your devotion, and your drive. My family buys businesses that need an injection of cash and new management to take them to a more profitable level. That is where we make money." He hesitated, "you have built this business from an idea and a desire to have a successful company and you are succeeding. All I do is work with what other people have built and then had issues or no desire to grow it anymore. You are absolutely and positively the opposite, I would never come between you and your business. I realise that something must have happened to you before that it is so difficult for you to trust, but I want you feel free to trust me."

"Lorenzo, don't ever think about trying to steal my business." Her voice was quiet which made her statement even more menacing.

"I keep telling you that your business is not what I want. Can't you hear what I'm saying? I just want you! Especially because in the short time we've known each other, I've fallen in love with you."

This comment did little to placate her, she recognised that she sounded unreasonable and wanted this conversation to be finished.

"Do you remember what I said I would do to you if you messed with me?"

"Yes, I remember."

"Remember this, it is not a threat. It is a promise."

For the first time in their short relationship, Lorenzo felt threatened and heard a seriousness in her voice that was unfamiliar to him. He could not believe that this was all happening over a simple compliment. Yet it was still insightful.

"Yvonne, as I said your business is very successful already, there is nothing I could bring or add to it. I have never met a businessperson with your dedication, intelligence, or business acumen."

He stopped to look into her eyes, he wanted her to see his sincerity. Then he continued, "so will you meet me at one o'clock today?"

"I'll think about it, and Lorenzo? I will honestly try to… to trust you."

Am I overreacting? I want to trust him, but… she could not think about it now.

He said nothing more, if she could not learn to trust him that would be the end of the relationship. As much as he might love her, trust was elemental and although Lorenzo Maldini was used to getting what he wanted, this determined and stubborn woman was decidedly a challenge. As he reflected on this, he went into the main office to find Gordon. She saw him approach Gordon's desk and fervently wished that she could hear the exchange between the two of them.

"Hi Gordon, I'm pleased to meet you." Lorenzo extended his hand and received a firm handshake from the man sitting at the desk, the only man in the office.

Gordon was in his late forties with decades of publishing experience behind him. His features belied his years, he was balding with sharp facial features and a rotund build around a short frame. Wearing his trademark checkered shirt, a whimsical tie and dark green suit, his trousers were supported by red braces. His brown brogue shoes were yet another of his trademark looks . He had been wearing this pair for almost ten years.

"Hello Lorenzo. I'm pleased to me you also and am entirely at your service." Gordon whipped a chrome fountain pen from out of his jacket pocket. A notebook had materialised on top of the desk, and he looked Lorenzo up and down. "Now tell me, will you be writing this book yourself? The boss hasn't filled me in yet."

"Gordon, there is as much chance of me writing the book as winning a gold medal at the Olympics. That English degree was the end of my writing career." Lorenzo found an empty office chair and pulled it over so that he could speak more comfortably with Gordon.

Gordon chuckled at the joke. "Looks like I'm going to be your ghost-writer then. We'll collaborate on the contents, but I'll do the actual writing. The best idea is to schedule a meeting to discuss the style of the health and fitness book structure, then I'll do some research and we will collaborate on content. You will review it for correct subject matter, and I will provide the creativity. How does that sound?"

Lorenzo nodded.

"Thinking about it," said Gordon pausing for a few seconds, "I'd like to structure in three sections, starting with a warm-up. The centre section could be exercise routines, and the end section could be a cool-down and relaxation section. The whole thing could be a mix-and-match concept. Coupling the book with a YouTube video channel that we can expand on in time to come is a huge road this company can explore with you as the lead instructor for future development."

Lorenzo was delighted with Gordon's suggestions, thanked him and stood up leaving the main office without looking back into Yvonne's private office. All the while her eyes were on him until the lift doors closed.

As she watched the clock hit half-past twelve, Yvonne wondered whether she should go see Lorenzo, as he had suggested. She had concentrated on the work which had been piling up on her desk, so at twelve forty-five, seeing a reduction in the mountain of paperwork and response to emails, she decided to go.

After taking public transport to Merchant City, she stood outside Lorenzo's building and pressed the buzzer for his flat.

"I'm on my way down," said Lorenzo in a tinny, distorted voice, not giving her a chance to speak.

"You're not letting me in?" This surprised her.

"No, no need." She heard the intercom click off and she waited at the entrance to the apartments until Lorenzo opened the door.

"Come on."

"Come on where?"

She did not know what state they were in, and she was still unsure about whether or not he could be trusted.

"With me," he said gently, taking her hand and leading her around the back of the block to the car park. "To stop you stealing my Range Rover."

Lorenzo pressed a set of keys into her palm, curling her fingers around them. When she opened her hand, she saw an electronic car key. It took her a moment to process what she was seeing, and when she touched the 'unlock' button on the key fob. The headlights on a bright red Audi with a YDP 1 licence plate flashed, briefly illuminating the car park.

"Are you kidding me?" she asked quietly.

She could not believe what she was seeing. After the way that she had spoken to him earlier that morning, she could not believe he was gifting her a car, and Audi at that.

"No. This is from me to you."

Her independent nature exploded. But not wanting another emotional scene she just stood looking at the car.

"Lorenzo this is silly. I can't take this," she stammered, overwhelmed by the generosity of the gesture.

"Okay, give me the keys back then." He held his hand out expectantly, but his eyes were glimmering with silent laughter.

Suddenly, she hesitated. "I changed my mind. I'll keep it. But honestly, why do you do these things, Lorenzo?"

He pulled her into a tight embrace. "Yvonne, please take it. It's only a car. A gift from me to you, for being you. I love you and I trust that you love me, and that is all that truly matters between us."

She smiled at his last remark, and the worries she had had only a few hours ago seemed to melt away. "Nobody has ever spoiled me the way that you do, or made me feel the way you do," she murmured against his chest.

He kissed her lightly on the forehead. "Well, you don't exactly make it easy."

Lorenzo jumped as he felt a strong pinch on his back.

"See what I mean!" He laughed. "The next stop is Sardinia, and I'll introduce you to my family, including my father, Il capo di tutti I capi."

"Okay," she said in a daze of ecstasy, still staring at her new car, oblivious to the meaning of what he had said.

Sliding into her extravagantly luxurious Audi, she felt the warmth of the heated leather seats, the softness of the steering wheel encased in leather, the hard leather grip on the gear lever and sighed with pure pleasure. She pressed the button to turn on the ignition, feeling the purr of the stationary engine and gazed at the monitor which provided every assistance from directions to parking and more to be discovered.

Reversing the car out of its parking space and turning toward the electronic gates, she realised she had a slight issue, and lowered the driver's window to ask, "Lorenzo, how do I get out of here?"

He leaned through the open window to hand her an access card to his apartment and fob for the car park.

"Oh, Lorenzo are you sure about this?"

"Trust me, I have never been more sure about anything in my life." He smiled reassuringly at her and waved at the rear window of the car.

The next day as Yvonne drove into the car park at her office, Gordon was shuffling papers at the window above, trying to work out where to start with the keep-fit project. He watched Yvonne get out of a brand-new Audi and his eyes narrowed as he read the number plate. He knew who that car was from, and he did not like it. Lost in thought, he did not hear the lift ding as the doors opened.

"It's Friday," announced Yvonne cheerfully, breezing through the main open space towards her office. "Team meeting please in five minutes."

Once they had all assembled in Yvonne's office, each with a to-do folder of tasks pertaining to their current projects, she announced that she would not be available again until Tuesday morning. Having quickly become accustomed to her usual behaviour, there were only a few curious murmurs among staff members. Only Gordon knew that there was some significance in that statement.

Once business was out of the way, everyone shuffled out to finish up their tasks before the end of the day and start of the weekend.

Gordon was the last to leave. "Nice car Yvonne. A gift?"

"Yes, as a matter of fact. Also, I will be leaving in about five minutes, so would you handle the office while I'm out? With Anne away, you're the one I trust the most. I just wanted to stop by to make sure that everyone was in good shape for the start of next week."

"You never leave early," he commented.

"Well, I am today." She paused as though wondering how to ask him her next question, without inviting too many of his own. "Gordon, you know everything. What's a Capo?"

"Why do you ask that?"

"Oh just something I heard."

Gordon knew that the word meant 'boss' in Italian, but he was reluctant to get involved in her private love affair.

"Sorry, Yvonne that's a new one for me. You'll have to search that one on the internet," and hurried to his desk.

Confused by Gordon's skittish behaviour, Yvonne pulled out her mobile to call Lorenzo. The phone rang until voicemail informed her Lorenzo was unavailable, so she left a quick message as she locked the drawers on her desk, rushing to leave the office.

"Bye everyone, have a great weekend. Last to leave please make sure to lock up," she instructed. Everyone watched her depart and no one questioned anything until she was out of earshot.

"Something's not right," commented Amy. "In all the years I have known her, she's never been like this. What do you think is going on?"

Gordon only shook his head. He did not know what to think.

Chapter Nine

Yvonne drove away in her new Audi to meet with Lorenzo and she felt she had met the love of her life. She was always very careful when choosing someone, as she did not want anyone who was only interested in going out with her because of her business success. The memories flooded back, her first small business set up as a partnership with her boyfriend. They had just signed a large contract and were celebrating, she remembered waking up in the morning with a huge headache and could not understand - she never had hangovers. Then it was a rush; boyfriend gone, money gone, and she had to take all her savings to finish the contract which finished her company.

With Lorenzo, it felt different. She was giddy with the intensity of their romance. Her heart pounded when she thought about him, she blushed when she remembered what they did together, and she smiled every time he looked at her. Here was someone who genuinely loved her.

Opening the door to Lorenzo's building using the card that he had given her, she made her way to his door. Although she technically had access, she was not the type to simply barge in. It was still his apartment, and she respected his space. Instead, she knocked on the door and waited for a reply.

As he opened the door for her, ushering her in, he asked, "Is your card not active? I gave it to you to use," he reassured her as he leaned forward with a smile and kissed her.

"I didn't want to just come in as if I owned the place," she admitted, kissing him back.

"Oh, Yvonne. You know you can come here anytime you like." He chided her as he headed towards the minibar.

From her seat on the settee, she called over to him, "I was looking at flights today. I see we have to go to London for a connection to Sardinia. Do you want to drive, or will we fly there?"

"Oh, don't worry about that, everything's already taken care of."

"Yes, you are good at getting everything taken care of," she joked.

Lorenzo flashed her a dashing smile. "Do you have your passport? Is there anything else you want to take with you?"

"I'm all packed and ready to go." Yvonne said, patting the small cream leather suitcase next to her that she had brought up from the car.

"Okay, great. We're getting picked up in about half an hour by a friend of mine, so would you like a glass of wine while we wait?"

"Yes, that would be lovely."

She watched as Lorenzo poured a deep red wine into a cut crystal glass, admiring the clothes that he was wearing. He was dressed in another tailored navy Armani suit, and he looked every inch a successful businessman. She could not decide if she preferred him dressed like this, or sweaty from the gym, or simply naked.

As he handed her a glass of a delectable Italian wine, he kissed her deeply. They sat together on the settee, their light-hearted whispers and giggles only interrupted by seductive kisses. They felt like young teenagers in love for the first time who could not wait to explore each other.

Suddenly, his mobile began to ring, jolting them back to reality.

"Hello?" answered Lorenzo. "Okay, we'll be right down." He hung up the call, then turned to Yvonne and declared that it was time to go as he lifted their bags.

When they arrived on the street, she saw a sleek black Mercedes with dark tinted windows and a uniformed driver waiting opposite the building.

"Good evening, madam," greeted the driver as he opened the door for her.

"Good evening to you," she replied as she slid into the back seat.

"Mr Maldini, sir. Nice to see you again."

"Nice to see you too, Vincent," he replied as the driver closed the passenger door behind them.

"Airport, sir?"

"Yes please, Vincent." Lorenzo looked over to see Yvonne staring out of the window

"What's up?" he asked, placing a hand on her thigh, stroking it with his thumb.

"Nothing," was Yvonne's simple reply, as she continued to stare out of the window as the car was driven onto the M8 towards Edinburgh Airport. "I thought we were heading for Glasgow Airport?"

"Yes, I know but all is good at Edinburgh Airport. Will you trust me Yvonne?"

She took a deep breath and decided to trust him. This relationship was too important to lose over her issues.

The car arrived at Edinburgh Airport about forty-five minutes later. Yvonne was confused as they turned away from the main terminal, instead, heading towards a small building where passport control had a separate office for executive air passengers.

Suddenly the engine was cut, and Vincent was stepping out of the front seat, holding the door waiting for both Yvonne and Lorenzo to get out. "I hope you both enjoy your flight."

"Thank you." Yvonne smiled as she stepped out of the car.

"Thanks, Vincent. See you Monday night?" asked Lorenzo, as he shook the chauffeur's hand.

"Yes sir." He got back into the car and drove away smoothly.

They walked towards a small building, passports in hand. As there were no other passengers, Yvonne tensed and finally whispered. "Lorenzo, what is all this?"

"It's the start of a long weekend in Sardinia with the lady I'm in love with." He looked over his shoulder at her, squeezing her hand in reassurance.

"This is madness, total madness!" she exclaimed. She could feel herself beginning to panic when she realised that their luggage had been left in the boot of the car, which was out of sight by now. Frustration caused her to stop in her tracks. "You do know you left our bags in the car?"

"No, I haven't. They're being loaded while we wait through here," he replied calmly.

"Passports please," requested the customs officer, tactfully ignoring Yvonne's anxiety. He examined both passports before returning them with a smile. "Enjoy your flight, your aircraft is ready."

"What aircraft?" Yvonne raised her eyebrows, looking at Lorenzo.

"The one sitting over there," he replied pointing to a jet with the initials LM intertwined on the tail.

She hung back, suddenly. "Lorenzo, I can't go with you."

"May I ask why not?" His tone was patient.

"Because this is way out of my league. This is all just too much for me. This kind of life… it just isn't… it isn't normal," her words rushing out with an onslaught of emotion. I just want a normal boyfriend!" Her voice was strained, lowering again into a whisper. *I like to be in control, and I am not with you,* were her unsaid words.

"I am normal, honestly," he reassured, his arms open as if pleading with her.

"Right! A private jet with your initials emblazoned across the tail. You call that normal?"

"You think this is mine?"

"Well?"

"Hell no, I just get to use it. LM doesn't always mean 'Lorenzo Maldini'. Come on, let's go," he laughed. He held his hand out to her and as he looked into her eyes with such love, she felt all her misgivings wash away and she smiled linking her fingers into his own.

Boarding the aircraft, she took her seat across from Lorenzo. Yvonne looked around the aircraft. The interior was exquisite, finished with beautiful soft furnishings. A plush cream carpet, light blue and cream leather seats with high backs and dark blue piping contrasted the dark mahogany veneered tables. There was seating for eight passengers, along with luxury amenities such as hot and cold water taps and ice dispensers. There was even an inflight entertainment centre with CD and DVD players. *This is a step above economy,* Yvonne thought to herself. Albeit a successful businesswoman, Yvonne was also down-to-earth and although she would splurge for a luxurious holiday it had never stretched to a private jet.

The door to the aircraft closed with the push of a button and after a short announcement, the pilot guided the aircraft onto the runway, and they were heading for Sardinia.

After they had been in the air for about twenty minutes, Yvonne broke the silence. "You need to speak to me, Lorenzo. Please," she asked softly, looking at him and taking his hand.

"I don't want you to feel uncomfortable, Yvonne." He ran his thumb over the back of her hand absentmindedly.

She waited for him to continue, which he did only after taking a deep breath.

"I've never done this before. Any time I've gone home, it's always been alone. I have never taken a woman to meet my family. We are so alike in the sense because I'm also very careful about who I go out with, and what they get to know about me." He looked at her intently.

"So…" she hesitated, digesting what it was that he was saying before she asked anything. "So, are you saying that you are not just a keep-fit instructor?"

"Yes, I am a keep-fit instructor but—"

"But what?" she interjected

"I'm also a Maldini. I am Lorenzo Maldini… and by the look on your face, that means absolutely nothing to you." He let out a low laugh, more pitiful than humorous.

"You're right, it means absolutely nothing to me." Confusion mounted as everything he said left her with more questions instead of answers.

"I'm so pleased that you know nothing about my family." He squeezed her hand as his shoulders relaxed.

"You know that I'm in love with you," her voice soft as her finger stroked the back of his hand.

"That's why you are sitting where you are," he said

"Ten minutes to landing sir," said the pilot from the cockpit.

"Thank you, Fabio." He turned back towards Yvonne. "Better buckle up, time to go down."

The aircraft touched down without a bump and turned into the executive parking bay at Olbia airport, near the Costa Smerelda in the northern part of Sardinia. Their bags were unloaded as they exited the plane, and they headed to check-in and have their passports checked.

"Mr Maldini! Benvenuto, nice to have you home," greeted the customs officer in Italian.

Although mystified at the exchange taking place as she knew no Italian, Yvonne handed her passport over for inspection. The customs officer looked between the photograph and the woman standing in front of him.

After a cursory glance, he smiled, returning her passport and in perfect English issued his simple greeting, "Welcome to Sardinia."

Yvonne returned the smile and replied with the only Italian she knew. "Grazie."

Once they were in the car park, Lorenzo took a set of car keys from his pocket, looked around and pressed on the key fob. The lights on a nearby Ferrari flashed in response.

"I suppose this isn't yours either."

"Yes and no. Yes, I can use it whenever I wish, but the title is not in my name."

"I'm still a bit nervous about all this, to be honest."

"Just relax and enjoy your weekend. Next stop, Porto Cervo," he announced as they drove off, accelerating quickly.

The evening sun was fading over the hillside in a spectacular blaze of orange, illuminating the idyllic scenery of Sardinia. They were driving lazily along a private road, enjoying their time together. Yvonne observed the extensive vineyards on either side of them, filled with grapevines that extended for several miles.

"Where are we Lorenzo?" she asked as the view rushed past.

"For you, a lovely villa for a weekend away. For me, home. Welcome to Maldini Estates."

"Oh my god!" she blurted out then quickly covered her mouth. *Does all of this actually belong to his family,* she wondered to herself.

The next few minutes passed in silence, Yvonne taking in the beauty of the countryside, before the car pulled up in front of a massive mansion. The doors swung open and the Maldini family rushed out to welcome their son home with wide-open arms. He stepped out of the car into a big family huddle, while Yvonne stood back watching them, giving them their moment of being reunited with their son and brother.

As she waited, she observed the pristine white house. Lights from within shone down onto the gravelled driveway with its white marble fountain, as well as the security lights which had been activated when Lorenzo drove in. Huge windows across the length of the front of the house overlooked the driveway and garden. The entrance had two massive carved pillars supporting a balcony that extended out from the main building. Large glass doors on the upper floor opened outwards onto the balcony, with ornate railings and offering expansive views across the vineyards. Contrasting the rest of the modern exterior, two heavy oak doors that looked like they dated back a few centuries opened into the house. The blend of old and new worked well to create an elegant and luxurious feel to the family home.

"Everyone, I want you all to meet Yvonne," announced Lorenzo in both Italian and English, as his family greeted her warmly.

Lorenzo took a moment to gesture to each of them as he made the introductions, "This is my mother, Sofia, my father, Leonardo, and last but not least, my sister, Maria."

As Yvonne shook their hands and received a traditional kiss on each cheek, she felt herself relax at last. Their obvious wealth was intimidating, but they seemed warm and welcoming.

Yvonne immediately warmed to Sofia, as she reminded her of her own mother. With beautiful, sparkling dark eyes a warm, welcoming smile, she was very petite with greying hair pulled into an old style chignon. Nothing about her suggested she was married to a very wealthy man. She was dressed simply and lacked the desperate need to avoid ageing so prevalent in the current society. *You would fit nicely in the West End of Glasgow,* Yvonne thought. She caught a flash of approval from Sofia to Lorenzo as they were introduced, which inexplicably filled her with warm pride.

As she turned to face Leonardo, Yvonne had an internal chuckle to herself as her mischievous side thought, *so this is what a Mafia boss looks like in real life…* just like someone's grandfather. Leonardo stood about six feet six inches tall, and incredibly slim. He was bronzed from head to toe, his Mediterranean skin glowing in the sunlight, and thick, pure white hair was slicked back across his head. His deep-set brown eyes were firmly locked on her as he evaluated his son's choices.

His open-necked white shirt revealed a thick gold neck chain with the initials 'LM' in the centre a sign of his lavish taste.

Then there was Maria. There was no doubt that Lorenzo had a great relationship with his sister and that she was the one he wanted approval in his choice of a girlfriend from. She was twenty-five and her beauty came from her extraordinarily bright blue eyes that contrasted with her luscious, dark wavy hair. She was dressed in a silken, midi-length flora dress that hugged her curvaceous figure in such a way that she looked both sultry and elegant. Her smile was dazzling and she reminded Yvonne of herself at the same age.

"So you are Yvonne then," remarked Maria. Her tone was cheery and Yvonne was desperate to get to know Lorenzo's bubbly little sister.

As Yvonne entered the house with Lorenzo by her side, all the trappings of wealth were evident. The entrance was grand and lavishly decorated.

"Please, this way," instructed Lorenzo's father, guiding her gently towards the lounge by her elbow. Large oil paintings hung from the walls, of the estate in years gone by. Despite that, they were not tacky, but rather an elegant tribute to the development of the Maldini home over the years. Golden sconces were evenly spaced between the paintings, casting a warm glow around the room. The whole effect was that of a warm welcome home, even if you were not part of the immediate family.

"Thank you, sir," she replied politely.

"Forget the sir, I am Leonardo,"

"This is so exciting," Maria gushed in perfect English, materialising next to her and linking arms.

"What is?" asked Lorenzo who was trailing behind the growing entourage.

"A woman in your life at long last," she replied over her shoulder.

Yvonne had never been in a house like this in her life. The lounge was massive with a marble staircase that ascended into a half landing before breaking off into two semi-circular staircases, one to the left and one to the right. There was a large crystal chandelier that sent sparkles across the ceiling. It was breathtaking.

Pure white, soft Italian leather settees were scattered about, with equally white Turkish silken rugs nestled between them. Another slightly smaller crystal chandelier lit the room, which when cast across the stark white decoration, was slightly blinding. A large marble fireplace adorned one wall, making it the centrepiece. *How much marble can one mansion have,* she wondered as they moved through the room. A beautifully scenic, but heavily framed painting hung directly above the fireplace. Leonardo watched Yvonne as she gazed at the painting.

"That, dear lady, is a painting of the Maldini Estate as it is today, I had the estate photographed from the air, then I commissioned an artist to paint what you see before you"

"It's beautiful." Yvonne breathed.

"Tomorrow in the daylight I'll give you the guided tour if that's alright with you?" Lorenzo asked as the main group dissipated.

"Yes, certainly. I am honestly stunned, Lorenzo, it is amazing,"

As the family busied themselves preparing the table for a feast, Yvonne glanced around then whispered to Lorenzo, "I need to speak to you."

"What about?" he asked quietly. As he leant in to hear her answer, she could smell him – a delightful and seductive combination of sandalwood, cedar wood, and amber.

"Em," she said, shaking her head to clear her mind. "Where are the bags?"

"In the car," he smiled at her.

"You are not getting my message here are you?"

"Oh right, that. We have our place just down the road. How does that sound?"

"Perfect." She sighed with relief.

They all sat down at the table in the dining area which formed part of the elongated open plan lounge, Yvonne was fascinated by the thick oak table, running her fingers along the grain of the wood. It was large enough to seat at least twenty people, with matching high-backed chairs carved with the letter 'M' placed all around. Set just away from the fireplace and settees, each area of the open room had a unique and distinct feel.

"What are you thinking?" asked Lorenzo quietly, watching her lovingly from the other side of the table.

"I'm thinking I have never seen anything like this before, this table is beautiful." Marred with small holes from woodworm, and softened with use, the table was unique and elegant, grounding the elaborate decor in the rest of the house.

"This is why my father is rich," Lorenzo laughed, "he gives nothing away. This is our old barn door. It even matches the casks that the red wine ferments in."

Yvonne took her place next to Lorenzo and stared at the spread that had been prepared for Lorenzo's homecoming and laid out by his mother. Two large candelabras sat on the long table, the flickering of the candles creating a relaxed ambience as the shadows danced across the walls.

Lorenzo saw that Yvonne looked a little astonished with the amount of traditional Sardinian food before her and immediately stepped in to put her at ease.

"Yvonne, let me introduce you to my mother's cooking and the delights you are about to savour." He began pointing to each of the platters on the table. "*Su Porcheddu*. Among the most famous meat dishes on the island, *Su Porcheddu* is better known as a roast suckling pig. Then we have *Culurgiones*. One of the tastiest pasta dishes in the whole of Italy, the pasta in *Culurgiones* is filled with a combination of potato, pecorino cheese, garlic, olive oil and mint leaves. This is *Pane Carasau*. This wafer-thin light bread is the classic Sardinian starter. *Pecorino Sardo* is the home cheese of Sardinia, and finally, we have *Seadas*. That is a dessert of sweet ravioli with fresh cheese, with honey and sugar over the top of the dessert."

Lorenzo's mother was pouring a vivid red wine into crystal glasses while Yvonne listened to the detailed explanation, she then took a sip and was delighted by the rich notes on her tongue.

Leonardo Maldini sat at the head of the table. Sofia was at his right-hand side and his daughter was to his left. Perched on the ends, Lorenzo sat next to his mother while Yvonne sat beside Maria.

Everybody was silent for a moment as they enjoyed the delectable spread in front of them. Yvonne was amazed at how delicious everything was, and the clinking of cutlery against crockery showed that everyone was enjoying it just as much as she was. Pleasant small talk interspersed the meal before Leonardo became more serious.

"Yvonne," he began, dabbing at the corner of his mouth with a napkin, "what is it about my son that attracted you to him?"

"Actually, Lorenzo pursued me. He was my personal trainer but expressed that he wanted a more personal relationship with me."

"You know he is a Maldini?"

Lorenzo looked at Yvonne and he knew what was coming.

Yvonne had her hands spread flat on the table as she began to adopt the attitude that made her so successful in business negations. "Mr Maldini," she said gazing firmly and confidently straight into his eyes. "All I knew about Lorenzo, up until we drove in here, was that he used to be my personal fitness trainer and that I love him. And I know he loves me too. That is all that matters."

He looked at her across the table as if weighing her up. He smiled and nodded. Lorenzo breathed a sigh of relief. Sofia and Maria smiled secretly behind their wine glasses.

"Are you from Glasgow?" he asked.

"Yes, I am."

"I lived there for years getting my business together, building a life for us, then I came back here to my home. All this has been in my family for generations, many generations in fact, and one day," he continued, gesturing to Lorenzo, "he is going to inherit all this." He looked pointedly at her, evidently not finished with his interrogation. "I would like to ensure that my son is not going to marry some gold-digging shop girl."

Lorenzo cringed as everybody looked at Yvonne in shock.

Yvonne's temper began to simmer yet there was a cold expression in her eyes and her mouth was set in a firm line. "If it wasn't for shop girls and others like them, then you would not have a business here or in Scotland for Lorenzo to inherit. You should learn to treat your staff with respect. I know I do," she stated in a calm and measured tone.

Leonardo turned to Lorenzo and said in Italian, "I like her, she has balls, taking me on like that," which resulted in both of them laughing.

Wanting to change the subject and take back some control that she had lost when the men started speaking Italian to each other, Yvonne turned and said, "Maria, your English is brilliant. Where did you learn?"

"Oh, I have Italian blood, but I'm born and bred Scottish."

"Oh, well did I mess that one up, Lorenzo, I blame you for not preparing me," she chastised with a teasing laugh. She tried again. "May I ask where the wine that we had tonight came from? I have to get some to take back with us."

"It's the family wine produced in our own vineyards, the ones we drove past. We keep it in the cellar downstairs," answered Lorenzo, laughing again.

"I give up," she sighed, throwing her hands up in a dramatic gesture as everyone collectively laughed.

All the time that the banter-slash-interrogation was going on, Sofia Maldini said nothing. Yvonne watched as she lifted and laid everything before her husband, her eyes downcast while he commanded the attention. As Sofia began to clear the table and take plates into the kitchen Yvonne excused herself and followed her.

"Thank you for dinner tonight, Mrs Maldini. It was delightful. May I help you with anything in here?"

Sofia looked sharply at Yvonne, who was surprised by the depth of emotion in her eyes. "He is wrong speaking to you as he did."

Yvonne was taken aback. "Mrs Maldini, please don't worry about it, I can handle myself."

Sofia Maldini was busying herself with the dirty dishes, her eyes trained downwards again. "Do you love my son?"

"Yes, very much."

"Then do not let my husband destroy what you have," she replied cryptically.

"I won't, but you have to believe me, I knew nothing about all this."

"I know," she said softly patting Yvonne's arm before leaving the kitchen. The whole encounter left Yvonne feeling puzzled.

They returned to the table and Lorenzo flashed a knowing look at Yvonne as his mother began to pour coffee for each around the table.

"Where are you both staying tonight?" asked Maria mischievously, breaking the deafening silence.

"Now that is a good question, where are we staying tonight darling?" Yvonne echoed with a dazzling smile as she looked towards Lorenzo.

"My place," Lorenzo replied knowing he had already told Yvonne that. "Speaking of, it's time we were heading out."

He thanked his parents in Italian for their hospitality, while Yvonne shook their hands and repeated his sentiments in English.

Maria led Yvonne from the house. "We have to get together this weekend," she said, hoping she would gain the sister she never had.

"I would love that."

They waved back at the house and the family standing outside. The engine of the Ferrari burst into life and within minutes, it was silent again outside a small cottage on the grounds of the Maldini estate. Lorenzo lifted the bags and led Yvonne into his house.

"You are the first woman ever to enter here, besides my mother and Maria of course," he commented as they set their bags down inside the slightly smaller version of the mansion they had just left.

"Why?"

"Because I have never been in love like this before, and you are so, so special." He swept her up into a tight embrace and showered her with kisses. He put her down, poured two glasses of the family wine and then they sat on the couch.

"You okay?" she asked.

Lorenzo remained silent for a minute or so. "Promise you won't tell anyone?"

Her curiosity piqued, she reassured him, "Of course I won't."

As Lorenzo snuggled into her, he broke his silence. "I love my mother and father, I love my sister, but I hate being a Maldini and everything it brings with it, to be quite honest."

"What do you mean?" she asked, stroking his lustrous dark hair back from his forehead.

"Everyone on this island knows us, and this is the reason that I'm in Scotland, I want to be free of all this," he explained, gesturing vaguely around him. There was silence between them. "Back home in Scotland, I am free. I am who I am there, not who I am here – son of Leonardo Maldini. Do you know what I mean?" he asked with a sadness in his voice that Yvonne had not heard before. "I love my father like any son loves his father, but, being a Maldini is a great strain, I just need to be free of all this here."

"Listen to me. I love you Lorenzo Maldini, the guy I met in Glasgow, and tomorrow you are taking me out and showing me around."

"Yeah, okay."

"Right there is something else I have to say to you," Yvonne said softly, as she stroked his hair. Six, eight, ten, whatever weeks ago, I came to your keep-fit class and here we are sitting in Sardinia, I don't even know how to describe it, Maldini paradise. There is something I want to ask you."

"Okay," he replied, wondering what was coming but fearing the worst.

"When we get back to Glasgow can we get back to being us?"

"What do you mean?"

"You working with Gordon on your book and the YouTube videos, me and you at Arthur's night club with all those females drooling over you and going to a small café with a band where this all started?"

"Will you be there with me?"

"Every step of the way" she replied.

Chapter Ten

The early morning Italian sunshine streamed through the bedroom window, welcoming a new day into their life together. Yvonne awoke on the most luxurious mattress she had ever slept on, set in a beautiful, antique, wooden bed frame. She slipped naked out of the bed and wrapping herself in Lorenzo's button-down Armani shirt she wandered around the cottage exploring.

The cottage had thick stone walls, painted white inside and out, contrasting with the red-tiled roof and creating a delightfully rustic atmosphere that was completely different to the vast expanse of the main mansion.

Moving through the rooms, Yvonne found herself in a kitchen where nineteenth-century Maldini taste clashed with twenty-first-century trends. She found herself in a well-fitted open plan kitchen with all the latest gadgets. *I could sure make an amazing fry-up in this kitchen,* Yvonne thought mischievously.

Inside the living room, a glass-fronted cabinet was filled with family memorabilia and the vintage light fixtures were from bygone days as was the timber-topped dining table; it all worked together to give the room a charm of its own. Looking up, the dark timber roof beams were exposed, as were the cross beams with everything bolted together. The atmosphere was wonderfully warm and cosy as if this was the real family home, not a guest house. Behind the sofa, Yvonne peered through a set of antique lace curtains, revealing an expansive patio with a large jacuzzi, set in a lush green garden. *This is outrageous,* she thought to herself as she threw open the doors, gazing into the clear blue water of the warm, bubbling jacuzzi. As she strolled back into the living room, she could not quite believe exactly where it was that she was staying.

"The coffee maker is on the worktop in the kitchen," came a sleepy, disembodied voice from another room.

Walking back into the bedroom, Yvonne spoke in a sultry voice. "My coffee maker is lying right here," wrapping herself around him as she got back under the covers. They stayed like that for a while, before Yvonne broke the silence. "Do you want to know something?"

"Yes, I want to know something."

Lying in his arms, she paused for a moment, thinking of the right words to say. "I do not want this lifestyle, any of this lifestyle at all."

"Are you telling me that we're finished?" he asked, slightly taken aback.

"No, of course not. All I'm saying is that when this weekend is over, I want us to go back home, back to our life. We don't need this extravagance, just as I said to you last night."

"Meaning what, exactly?"

"Me pinching your Range Rover, going out, having fun, things like that. I want to build a life with you, one that doesn't rely on your family influence."

He frowned as he digested what she was saying. "Yvonne, I love you, and I'm old enough to keep my family out of our relationship."

"Yes, I know, but we have to get back to being us," snuggling close to Lorenzo to emphasise her point.

"I agree. I just have to be here this weekend. I wanted you to see what you're getting into. While I'm not actively involved in my family life over here, it's still part of who I am."

"I am getting into nothing other than you," she replied flirtatiously. As she kissed him, she whispered, "coffee maker, time for coffee" against his neck, then added, "one thing, I do rather enjoy sleeping on silk sheets... maybe we can take those with us?"

After their slow morning, Lorenzo held his hand out. "Come with me, we're going for a walk," he said as he led Yvonne outside. Hand in hand, they meandered amongst the grapevines in the adjoining fields, as Lorenzo explained that his family had been involved in the winemaking business for a several generations, specialising in a few wines. "Here we call the beautiful red wine that these grapes produce cannonau, elsewhere it's called grenache. In the other fields that you can see, we have cabernet sauvignon and carignan. When we go back to the house later and stand on the balcony, you'll get the grand view of this place."

"It's truly beautiful," she replied as they strolled through the vineyards before returning to the cottage.

Soon after their return, there was a knock at the door, and Maria entered without waiting for a reply.

"Fancy a girly day?" She asked as she made herself at home at the dining table, picking up an apple from the abundant fruit display and tossing it into the air as she waited for a reply.

"Have to ask your brother about that one, I don't know if he has anything planned." Yvonne winked.

"Lorenzo, where are you?" shouted Maria, before biting into the apple.

"Here! Relax Maria, there's no need to yell. What is it?" Lorenzo appeared in the living room from the bedroom.

"Yvonne and I are going out for a while," announced Maria linking arms with Yvonne daring him to say no to her.

"Where are you going?" he asked inquisitively narrowing his eyes playfully at his sister.

"Porto Cervo."

"Yeah, okay," he replied. He kissed Yvonne delicately on the cheek. "Have fun."

"Yay! Let's go, girly day out." She threw the half-eaten apple into a tucked away bin and grabbed Yvonne's hand.

As they rushed outside, Yvonne looked at Maria's car.

"A Fiat?"

After the ostentatious displays of wealth that were prevalent in every aspect of Maldini life that she had seen over the past twenty-four hours, this was absurdly… normal.

"Yeah, this is my about-town car," replied Maria nonchalantly over the roof of the car.

"Don't tell me, your other one is a Ferrari?" joked Yvonne.

"Oh god no, it's a Maserati," replied Marie her tone nonchalant as she slid into the driver's seat.

Driving into Porto Cervo, Yvonne's eyes were roaming everywhere, studying at the expensive cars and yachts sitting in the purpose-built marina.

"As you can see, we're overlooking the marina and if we walk down there you'll see the houses that have been built in the typical Costa Smeralda style in the alleys, with their beautiful arched windows and little balconies. Welcome to Millionaire's Paradise."

Ditching the car in a side street Maria continued in her role as guide. "Usually, this place just has a couple of hundred residents but in the summer you find all sorts of film stars going about the small alleys. Is there anything you would like to see in particular?"

"I shall let you take the lead. You know the place."

"How about grabbing a coffee and we can get to know each other, for a start?"

Maria led them down one of the many narrow alleyways that led from the marina into the town, looking for a small, traditional café. Eventually, they found one and as they were watching the world go by.

Maria asked, "Who's going to go first?"

Yvonne sat pondering the question for a moment. "Me I suppose." She paused. "May I ask you something?"

"Sure," said Maria, "go for it."

"What do you know about me?"

Maria smiled. "I know that my brother loves you to bits. Other than that, not much. Lorenzo was obviously enjoying being selfish and keeping you to himself."

Yvonne's face reflected her joy as she looked at Maria. "That is so lovely to hear."

She looked down into her coffee cup before continuing.

"So," she began, "your dad thinks I work in a shop, which I assume means he thinks I have nothing going for me. He's wary of me."

Yvonne looked over at Maria, who simply shrugged her shoulders.

"So what if you do work in a shop, who cares? I have never seen my brother so happy."

"Maria, I own a company in Glasgow – Yvonne Duncan Publications. It's my own company. I have several employees, I own my own flat outright, I'm a very independent woman and I don't need anyone... other than your brother to keep me fit," she joked. "See all this," she gestured around her, "the plane, the cars, the house. It all means nothing to me. I started with absolutely nothing. I'm not rolling in cash like you lot, but I'm going to tell you something. Your brother means the world to me. I'm not in it for... whatever assets his family has, I'm in it for him. He has something special about him. I would kill for him." She stared directly at Maria to help with the sincerity of her statement.

Maria sat back in her seat inspecting Yvonne from head to toe. "Do you know something? I believe you, and I would love you as a sister-in-law. You are feisty," she laughed.

"Whoa!" Yvonne almost choked on her coffee. "We are light years from marriage."

Maria tapped her chin thoughtfully, as she debated how much information to divulge. "Do you know he's arranged a family party for you tonight?"

"No!"

"So now you know, but please you have to act surprised when you get there," whispered Maria with a conspiratorial wink.

"Okay, okay. I know nothing about it, I promise I won't say anything."

Yvonne sat pondering what this party could be about. Why did Lorenzo keep it a secret from her?

Maria nodded. "Now may I ask you something?"

"Sure," answered Yvonne as she sipped her coffee.

"Do you love Lorenzo?"

"I already told you that I do."

"Just checking. Now, let's go walkabout." They stood up and left their payment on the table.

"Porto Cervo," explained Maria, continuing her role as a tour guide, "translates to 'Deer's Port' and it's in the province of Sassari. There was a guy called Prince Karim Aga Khan, he and a couple of others created this place. We have shops, bars, and do you know they say this is one of the most expensive places in the world to visit, let alone live."

"So, say I want to buy a house here – what would it cost me?"

"Starting about three to three-hundred-and-fifty-thousand euros, or thereabouts, depending on the size of flat you're looking at," she answered casually. "Hotels cost a fortune to stay in here. One of them, I can't remember which one, was in the James Bond movie, 'The Spy something'."

"'The Spy Who Loved Me?'" suggested Yvonne.

"That one. Way before my time," confirmed Maria. "Right, let's go shopping."

As they strolled around window-shopping, everywhere was filled with luxury items, Yvonne noticed the world's top designers had a shop here and stopped at each one for a few minutes. "To be truthful Maria I've never owned anything like this."

"Oh, it's all that way here," replied Maria. "Listen, if you have to ask about the price, then you can't afford it," she said, without skipping a beat, "There's someone I want you to meet." She took Yvonne's hand and marched her into a shop across the street, with large windows and a chic display.

Maria began with the introductions. "This is Anastasia, my very favourite dress designer. Anastasia, this is Yvonne, Lorenzo's girlfriend."

"Hi," said Yvonne, "pleased to meet you."

"Ah, Yvonne. Lovely to meet you. Please wait here for a moment," greeted Anastasia in a lovely sing-song voice, and the most endearing Italian accent. She floated gracefully through to a room marked 'Private', before reappearing with a large, decorated box.

"Signorina, I have this for you," said Anastasia handing Yvonne the box which contained a simple, sleeveless, low-cut silk snowy white dress. While she had been admiring the stunningly elegant garment in front of her, Anastasia had produced a matching, slightly smaller box. "I have had these delivered for you here also," handing over the shoebox.

As Yvonne lifted the dress out of the box and held it in front of her, she turned to Maria and said, "This is stunning! So are those!" She exclaimed, looking into the shoebox which contained a pair of handmade, white leather high heels.

"Well, obviously Lorenzo has done his homework. Now you just have to try everything on."

"Maria…" protested Yvonne.

"Please, just try it on with the shoes," begged Maria as Anastasia ushered Yvonne into a fitting room set into the left-hand wall of the shop.

A few moments later, Yvonne appeared on the shop floor in her new figure-hugging dress from behind the changing room curtain.

Maria had a broad smile across her face which reflected in the mirror as Yvonne admired herself.

"I cannot believe this" Yvonne, turned this way and that to inspect the outfit from all angles. "It's stunning." She felt beautiful.

"Your red hair, your figure, that dress. Everything just goes together beautifully. You're going to be the belle of the ball," grinned Maria.

Yvonne reluctantly went back into the changing room to change. When she emerged back into the main room, Anastasia carefully folded the dress before placing it back into its box. She placed both boxes inside a large paper bag emblazoned with the designer's logo.

"Enjoy your dress and shoes. The bill has already been settled by Mr Maldini."

"I cannot thank you enough."

"Anastasia," said Maria cheekily, "I might need a dress for a wedding soon."

"Well, let me know when you need it and I will make you beautiful."

Yvonne and Maria left the shop, heading back out into the warm Italian sunshine.

"Time we got back to the cottage. There's a party that you know nothing about to get ready for Yvonne."

Yvonne turned and wrapped her arm around Maria's shoulder in a close sisterly hug.

As Maria dropped Yvonne off, her parting comment was, "hey, future sister-in-law, see you tonight. Slay them in your new outfit."

Yvonne waved, then went into the cottage to find Lorenzo.

"Oh, you're back then." Lorenzo was sitting at the kitchen table. He shut his laptop which he had been working on and came to greet Yvonne with a kiss.

"This family is so lovely! I love your sister and your mum, but your dad? Now, he is a challenge, but I can get around him no problem. Watch this space," she exclaimed confidently.

"Have you been shopping?" he asked with a smile as he saw her matching boxes.

"Yes, and I honestly don't know how to thank you for my dress and shoes." She could not stop smiling, she felt as if she was walking on clouds.

"I will think of something, but that's for later," he replied with a cheeky grin.

She laughed as she wrapped her arms around his neck in delight.

"Yvonne, you ready to go to meet the family?" called Lorenzo.

Yvonne appeared. Her make-up was subtle except for bright red lipstick and a slight hint of winged eyeliner reminiscent of old Hollywood glamour. Her long red hair was curled for the occasion and the white dress hugged her beautiful hourglass figure. Her matching high heels clicked only slightly as she floated towards Lorenzo, feeling fashionable and elegant.

"Hells bells! You look absolutely… Geez, I don't know what to say. You're breath-taking."

"You don't look so bad yourself, Lorenzo." Sidling up to him to receive a kiss.

"Well, we now look the part, so let's do this," he said confidently.

"Yeah, let's do this," she echoed.

She glanced around the driveway at the parked cars, everything was top of the range, Ferraris, Alfa Romeos, Mercedes, Audi, and BMW, were all there.

"Right you, here we go," said Lorenzo.

"Lorenzo, do you think that this mob is going to get to me? No chance, I am a Glesga burd."

Lorenzo burst out laughing, "I don't know how to answer that"

Hand in hand they walked into the party. They were the clearly the stars of this show, as the Maldini's welcomed home their son, but Yvonne was there to make her presence felt one way or another.

Leonardo and Sofia welcomed their son and Yvonne into the party with exuberant greetings, embracing them warmly and planting hearty kisses on both cheeks.

As they all made their way inside, Yvonne was once again overwhelmed by the sheer luxury of Lorenzo's family home. The huge open plan lounge suddenly seemed small when it was filled with the Maldini relatives and friends. Orchestral music was playing in the background, through the surround sound speakers. Small groups milled about, chatting to each other, adding to the noise. Every one of them was immaculately dressed, the men in dark tailored double-breasted suits, and the woman in bright colourful cocktail dresses. Every so often, Yvonne would catch a flash of a huge diamond ring, used as another sign of their significant wealth.

The old barn door table that had hosted their evening meal the night before was once again laden with the Sardinian specialities as well as multiple bottles of wine from the family vineyards ensuring that not a single glass remained empty.

Some groups had found themselves outside around the swimming pool, where there was dance music thumping through the speakers, creating a livelier atmosphere.

Over the next hour or so, accompanied by Maria and Lorenzo, Yvonne was introduced to many family members and close friends. There was a slight language barrier, but they were both quick to translate for her. The wine from the family vineyards was flowing, everybody was mingling, and Yvonne was warmly received by those she had been introduced to which pleased Lorenzo. Yvonne felt she was making a good impression.

Lorenzo took Yvonne's empty glass from her and went over to the table for a refill, leaving Yvonne alone.

"Come with me," whispered Leonardo to Yvonne. It was more of an order than a request.

"Why?" she asked raising her voice slightly, but not enough to attract attention. She kept a professional smile plastered across her face.

"Because I said so," was his terse reply. She turned around to face him properly.

"Listen to me. I am not your wife, and I am not one of your servants, so ask me properly."

"Lorenzo, come here, get her into line," Leonardo commanded in Italian.

"You have no chance with her, father. She'll stand her ground."

Yvonne looked between the two of them unaware of what was said.

Leonardo switched back to English. "Both of you, come to my office." Yvonne was staring back at him. "Please?" he added begrudgingly.

"Not a word you're used to using," she mocked as she breezed past him.

They followed Leonardo into his office and she watched as he sat on a fine leather chair behind a large mahogany desk. The floor was made of more Italian marble, and the small crystal chandelier that hung from the ceiling caused it to sparkle. Three of the walls were oak-panelled, with a large family portrait hanging directly behind Leonardo. The remaining wall was primarily made up of three large windows that filled the room with natural light. She and Lorenzo sat on a set of magnificent matching red leather chairs on the opposite side of the desk. Lorenzo took Yvonne's hand, giving it a gentle squeeze of reassurance.

Leonardo leaned forward and took a large cigar from a Spanish Cedar wood box, then leaning back, he lit the cigar he gazed at the circular smoke rings floating above him. Then he turned his attention and looked directly at the couple.

"I think I am going to take a risk," began Leonardo Maldini breaking the silence and speaking in English to include Yvonne.

"Meaning what, Father?"

"I am thinking of going into publishing. Books, magazines, things like that, and with my contacts, it will go across Europe and into parts of America."

"Wait a minute," said Lorenzo, leaning forward, "where is this conversation going?"

"Your girlfriend drives a new Audi with the licence plate YDP 1, her company carries her name, I know that she is Yvonne Duncan Publications."

At this point, he turned to face Yvonne. "You are no more a shop girl than I am. I know absolutely everything about you, Yvonne."

He paused for a few minutes, puffing on the cigar then announced, "I want to buy your company." As a statement of intent, there was little tolerance for negotiation.

"It's not for sale," she defied quickly and politely.

"Everything in this world has a price. Tell her, Lorenzo."

"Everything has a price, Yvonne," he echoed reluctantly.

Yvonne glared at Lorenzo in disbelief, feeling angry and hurt. She was being sold down the river and all she could think was, *is this why I was brought all the way here?*

"Okay, Mr Maldini, please continue."

Yvonne assumed her poker face and confidently switching into business mode. Her open palms rested on her legs, and she stared directly at Leonardo with calm assurance.

"What are you asking for Yvonne Duncan Publications?" He puffed on the end of his cigar confidently.

Without hesitation, she replied, "the entirety of Maldini Estates for Maria and Lorenzo, with immediate effect."

"That is absolutely crazy!" exclaimed Leonardo.

He sprang up from his chair as if it had turned into hot coals, slamming the desk in anger. As he remained standing above them, he puffed on his cigar he to regain his composure.

"Okay, listen to me, Yvonne, Maria and Lorenzo will inherit all this one day, as I did, but not while I am breathing." He slowly lowered himself back into his chair to bring the negotiation back onto a level playing field.

"That is a shame." Yvonne shook her head mockingly. "It just means that you don't get my company."

She stood up, turned to leave, and glanced back at Leonardo as he sat back in his chair watching her. She gave him a small smile then opened the door leading into the large lounge and left ,followed swiftly by Lorenzo.

Lorenzo thought to himself, *is she joking about her price?* He also knew that she was a hard-nosed, feisty businesswoman, yet he could not help wondering what she was playing at.

"Why did you ask my father for Maldini Estates in return for your business?" whispered Lorenzo to Yvonne as the party around them got a little louder. "You know you have done yourself no favours with him by demanding that."

"I was once told by my grandfather, 'never answer a question with a question,' so to answer your question I considered it logically. I know your father is fabulously rich and would probably pay me in cash whatever I asked for my company, but I also know he cares about his kingdom as much as I care about my company, so I knew he would never agree to my price."

Lorenzo's smile indicated that she was right in her assessment.

"Now, as you have said, I may have done myself no favours with your father, but more importantly, where does that leave me with you? And us as a couple?"

"Exactly where we were before we went into that room. Nothing has changed for me."

Lorenzo brushed her forehead with his lips then turned to look around the room. "There is somebody I want you to meet though, and please try to get along. My cousin, Giovanni. He's been in New York for years but is now living in Glasgow. I think he may be living somewhere near to you. He hasn't arrived yet, but I think you'll like him."

Yvonne looked at Lorenzo, her eyes widening in apprehension. Her mind was in overdrive and butterflies began to rise in her stomach. She wondered, *could Giovanni be my stranger?*

Chapter Eleven

"I heard what you said to our father when he offered to buy your company," whispered Maria with a slight laugh as she stood shoulder to shoulder with Yvonne, scanning her relatives dotted around the room, her keen eyes taking everything in. "I'll admit I was eavesdropping and I think your asking price was brilliant!" Giving Yvonne's shoulders a congratulatory squeeze she continued. "People rarely decide to take him on, and I'm so impressed that you did."

"Yes, I was polite but I'm absolutely not ready to give up my company. Who knows what will happen in the future though." Yvonne answered absent-mindedly as she also scanned the room, but for one specific person.

"Yvonne, see when he wants something, he usually gets it." Maria cautioned.

"Well, I gave him a price and he declined to pay it." replied Yvonne defiantly.

Deciding to change the subject and put her rising anxiety at ease, Yvonne turned. "Maria, who is Giovanni? Lorenzo said he wanted me to meet him."

"Oh, he's my cousin, we all call him Gio. Spent years and years in New York, he was practically brought up there. He's been living in Glasgow for a couple of years though, working for a New York production company. It might even be his company, I'm not sure. They produce and promote music, so he's always travelling somewhere. I'm surprised that it's taken Lorenzo this long to introduce the two of you."

"Maria, are you employed, or have I forgotten what you already told me?"

"No, you've never asked, and I never told you," Maria quipped back, a feminine version of Lorenzo's smile flashing across her face.

"Well, are you going to tell me, or do I have to drag it out of you?" Yvonne smiled in return.

Maria answered as they wandered through the throng of people towards the bar that was set up in front of the fireplace.

"I run Maldini Estates, primarily focusing on the vineyards, overseen by my father. This is me in training to take over from him in the future."

"That's a lot of responsibility. What about Lorenzo?" Yvonne's inquisitive nature was beginning to take over.

"He takes care of everything else that is in Scotland."

Yvonne could see Maria was bored of the interrogation about her family dynamics as she was closely inspecting each perfect pink nail and they waited for two glasses of the full-bodied ruby wine to be poured.

She powered on her curiosity piqued. "What do you mean 'everything else in Scotland'?"

Maria glanced at Yvonne furtively. "Has Lorenzo not told you? We have a few other business ventures, just things that my father gets interested in. We have Italian clothing shops in Glasgow and various other cities, like Edinburgh and Aberdeen. And do you know that restaurant chain, Green's? My father owns that too."

The enormity of their empire was only just dawning on Yvonne as she slid onto the nearby settee. Looking concerned, Maria sat down next to her. After making sure that she was alright, she glanced hastily around the room, before lowering her voice.

"Don't say anything please, but the clothing chain is up for sale." Maria looked at her imploringly.

"Is it not lucrative enough?" asked Yvonne facetiously as she was surrounded by opulent evidence.

"Oh, hell yes. It's just that we don't have the time to look after it properly."

Maria changed the subject, and then after few minutes of polite non-invasive chatter, Yvonne excused herself to consider what she had learned as she stared at the large infinity pool purposely built to overlook the vineyards that stretched far into the horizon.

As she held a glass of the family red wine, she felt Lorenzo's arm slip around her waist and draw her close.

"How are you enjoying it?" he asked softly.

"At the risk of repeating myself, it's stunning here," she responded just as softly. Their heads were close together and she took comfort in leaning against him.

"Let's sit," suggested Lorenzo, pointing to a cushioned double seat at the pool's edge.

The throng of people that had been poolside upon their arrival disappeared inside and the thumping dance music from the speakers was replaced by a more soulful sound. As they sat side by side, they looked out across the rolling acres of Maldini Estates. The sun was setting in a glorious blaze of summer orange, reflected by the glittering blue water of the infinity pool and everything felt peaceful.

Yvonne hated to break that peace, but she needed to put her mind at ease. "There's something I need you to answer truthfully, Lorenzo... Did you know that your father was going to offer to buy my business?"

"No, absolutely not," he denied immediately.

Yvonne knew he was telling the truth by the vehement tone of his voice and how he looked directly at her.

"Thank you. I just needed to know." She reached across and squeezed his hand.

"Do you honestly think that I would have arranged all this for a bid on your own company?" His eyes were downcast, wounded at her lack of trust.

"Lorenzo, I don't know anything anymore," she sighed. "Your family is in a very different league." Her voice had a sad ring to it as she voiced what she had thought from the moment they arrived on the island.

"Does that include me?" he asked, fearing the worst. She started to reply but he interjected quickly. "See before you answer that, I want to tell you something." He faced her directly, holding her hands and maintaining eye contact to help her know how sincere he was being. "I love you and I would give all this up for you in a heartbeat."

"You would do that for me?"

"Do you want me to prove it?"

Yvonne pondered the question for a few silent moments, her arms folded in front of her. Laughter and music floated out from the main room, but the couple was so far removed from the party that they did not hear it.

"Okay, go on, prove it," she challenged him.

"Maria!" shouted Lorenzo, seeing that she was close by in the lounge. "Get yourself out here, please!"

Compelled by the urgency of his tone, Maria made her way over to where Lorenzo and Yvonne were sitting and stood with her back against the glass partition between the patio edge and the sheer drop to the vineyards below.

"What do you want, Lorenzo?"

"This is yours. In the future, everything is yours," he announced, gesturing around him.

"What the hell are you talking about?" replied Maria, taken aback. Her jaw dropped as the reality of what he had just offered her sank in.

"Well, I just told Yvonne that I would give all this up for her, which I've done. It's yours. So having done that, there is only one thing left to say."

Yvonne watched as Lorenzo stood up, moved in front of her and went down on one knee. Maria stood at the side with her mouth hanging open in a little 'o'.

Lorenzo reached into his jacket pocket and slowly produced a small, blue velvet box, held shut with an elegant gold clasp. He opened it to reveal a stunning four-carat solitaire engagement ring flashing the colours of the setting sun. He took it out of the box and held it up to Yvonne in his left hand.

She gasped.

"Yvonne Duncan. Will you marry me?" Lorenzo gazed into her eyes with love shining from his own.

Both Lorenzo and Maria were waiting for her reply, which seemed to take an eternity. Maria had her hands clasped over her face. Lorenzo just stared.

Everything around them seemed to occur in slow motion, while her heart was racing at one million miles an hour.

"May we live in Glasgow?" she asked, her voice breathy with excitement.

"We can live wherever you want to." A smile beginning to creep across his face.

"Then the answer is yes!" she cried ecstatically.

Tears of joy pooled in the corners of her eye as Lorenzo beamed and slid the ring onto Yvonne's finger. They embraced and kissed passionately, and the setting sun over the vineyards lit up behind them as if they both had halos. It was a perfect fairy-tale moment.

Maria was laughing and crying as she wrapped her arms around both of them, attracting the attention of those that remained at the family party.

"What is the problem out here, what is all this fuss about?" griped Leonardo in Italian, rushing to the poolside.

"Lorenzo and Yvonne are engaged!" Maria announced in English, and then again in Italian, to anyone who would listen.

Relatives gathered around offering congratulations to the happy couple.

Conversely, Leonardo glowered at his son. "Come with me now, Lorenzo," he demanded. Lorenzo sighed and resigned himself to following, but not before he gave Yvonne another kiss. Meanwhile, Maria had her arms wrapped around her future sister-in-law, glowing with as much happiness as Yvonne.

"Did you know anything about this?" asked Yvonne

"Listen, I'm an Italian woman who knows when an Italian guy is in love. I knew it was just a matter of time," she gushed, joy written all over her laughing face. "This means champagne and lots of celebrating? It's the only appropriate way to acknowledge your engagement!" she exclaimed.

Yvonne giggled, drunk with pure happiness. "I think we're already a little tipsy, Maria. But yes, back in Glasgow when we get away from all this, promise you'll come to visit?" Yvonne hugged her tightly.

"Done deal," answered Maria, hugging her back.

While it was a joyous celebration in the lounge it was a raging argument between father and son in the office.

"Father, see all this, leave it to Maria, do what you want with it, I don't need it! And more importantly, I don't want it!"

"This has been in the Maldini family for generations!" Leonardo raged, banging his fist on his desk. The solid door did nothing to soundproof his anger, and partygoers began to crowd around outside, listening intently to the drama unfold.

"Well, Maria is a Maldini too, so it's hers. It will still be in the family. I have Yvonne who is more important. If you don't like it, all I can say is that I am sorry that you are losing out on a beautiful, intelligent woman as a daughter-in-law."

"Beauty and intelligence do not go together, you stupid boy," Leonardo seethed.

"Father, with all due respect, get your head out of your arse and the nineteenth century," Lorenzo snapped.

He rarely had the balls to speak to the capo this way, but no one insulted his woman. After a moment, Leonardo spoke to his son in an uncharacteristically quiet icy tone.

"Don't tell me what to do. I am the head of this family until I die."

The unbridled rage had calmed into menacing authority, but Lorenzo was undeterred.

"Yeah, you always make sure that I know you're the capo of the Maldini clan!" Lorenzo declared sarcastically as his father opened a drawer on his desk, pulling out a handgun and pointing it at Lorenzo, who was suddenly stunned into silence.

The gravity of the situation had him frozen in his seat, paralysed by fear. They were suddenly interrupted and Leonardo looked up as his office door began to open following a short knock.

"Hey guys, what's going on?" greeted Giovanni in his New York drawl, pausing in the entryway when he spotted Leonardo with the gun in his hand. "Looks like I've arrived at a bad time. Or maybe right on time, depending on how you look at it."

He surveyed the scene before him but did not attempt to diffuse the situation. He swaggered into the room as if he owned the place, walking behind the desk to shake Leonardo's hand respectfully. "Uncle Leo, how are you?"

Lorenzo took this distraction as an opportunity to leave without angering Leonardo even more.

"Excuse me, father, I have a fiancée to see to." He held his head up and his shoulders back as he left the room, a picture of strength, but his breath was caught in his throat and sweat had gathered on his palms.

Looking at the door in disgust, Leonardo threw the handgun back into its drawer. "Gio, what do you have for me?" he demanded.

"I know you want Yvonne's company.

"Gio, you state the obvious!"

Gio wandered around the office knowing he was increasing the tension, then turned and smiled.

"I just happen to know a weakness. One you can decidedly exploit."

"Which is what, exactly?" Leonardo puffed on his cigar having reverted to his regular cold, calculating persona. Such an outburst of emotion was unusual for him.

"A part of her life that Lorenzo knows nothing of – she leads a double life." His tone was flippant, but he was holding his breath.

"Spare me the details," groaned Leonardo, rolling his eyes. "What do you want?"

"Oh Uncle, I will think of something. Now, what do you want from her? I'll get it for you."

"Gio, I have had her company examined in detail. It's on its way up, she has a good business model which is successful. And after that, I want to destroy every part of her life! So, Lorenzo will regain his senses and take his proper place with the family!"

"So, again, what do you want? The groundwork has been done." Giovanni leaned against the desk as if bored by the conversation.

Leonardo sat behind his desk, his finger slowly tapping out a rhythm as though he were listening to a song in his head. Several minutes later, the silence was broken.

"Meet her and give her this ultimatum; meet me, or reveal all to Lorenzo."

"Yes, Uncle," Giovanni replied as he left the office.

Chapter Twelve

Lorenzo walked through the house and he saw Yvonne deep in conversation with Maria out by the infinity pool. The warm night air made outside pleasant, even with an evening breeze.

"Yvonne, we need to go now!" His tone was urgent and he did not care that he was interrupting them.

"Go where?" She was bewildered

"Please just come, I'll explain on the way. Maria, my sister, I love you. See you soon," he said as he led Yvonne away.

"Yvonne, I'll phone you," called Maria, her voice raised and rather anxious about what could have caused this sudden departure.

"Lorenzo, please. What is going on?" Yvonne demanded as she was being dragged through the grand foyer.

"Same as usual, my father wanting to rule the roost over everyone, including me. I don't need it."

Lorenzo slammed the car doors shut and began the drive to the cottage. Gravel and dust were kicked up into a billowing cloud as the Ferrari sped away, obscuring the few family members who had curiously wandered to the entrance of the mansion.

"Well then, what are we going to do now?" asked Yvonne.

"Grab our bags and head home."

They did just that. Within two hours they had boarded the private jet and were in the air heading back to Glasgow.

Back at the Maldini household, Giovanni was catching up with various relatives that he had not seen for some considerable time, distributing hearty cheek kisses and firm handshakes amongst partygoers, before going for a walk around the property, looking for Lorenzo and Yvonne. He intended to meet them while they were together, to see what kind of reaction he would get from her when she found out who he was. He was certain that either Lorenzo or Maria would have mentioned their favourite cousin to her.

After a lap around all of the party areas, he had yet to find them.

"Maria, have you seen Lorenzo and Yvonne?" Giovanni quizzed nonchalantly as he circled back around to the bar.

"Yeah, they left here about an hour ago, maybe a little longer, after speaking with Father."

Giovanni's mouth twisted in frustration. "Do you know where they've gone?" He kept his voice calm, not wanting to alert his cousin to anything suspicious.

"No, but they are due to come back tomorrow before going home," she said looking at Giovanni, wondering why he was asking. "Is everything all right, Gio?" she asked as she accepted yet another glass of wine.

"Yes, of course. I can just catch up with them in the morning."

In the early hours of Sunday morning, Lorenzo and Yvonne landed in the exclusive executive area of Edinburgh airport. On the flight, Lorenzo had dialled Vincent and frantically explained the situation, and he was waiting for them in a freshly pressed uniform, despite the short notice. Having cleared immigration and customs, they drove down the M8 back towards Lorenzo's flat in the Merchant City. He needed a haven, somewhere he felt secluded after the stress of Sardinia.

"Well, that was a pretty sensational forty-eight hours of my life." Yvonne stood in the lounge with her hands on her hips, looking at her lover.

"I don't want you to get bored with me," he joked, with a tremor to his voice. He had to hide how shook up he was, so he focused his attention on her humorously.

"I don't think that is going to happen in a hurry." She smiled and walked towards him, bending over putting her hands on the arms of his seat. She kissed him gently, whispering, "I love you. Take me to bed please." She could sense that something was off and wanted to distract him, but also herself from the shocking revelation of who Giovanni was.

Yvonne awoke to the incessant ringing of her mobile phone. Lorenzo was asleep beside her.

"Hello?" answered Yvonne groggily.

"Yvonne, it's Maria. Where are you, are you coming to the house for breakfast?"

"Maria, we're back in Glasgow. I am so sorry I never got a chance to say goodbye to you or your family. I feel so bad about it."

There was a moment of silence as Maria processed this information. "Why are you there?" she asked, disappointment apparent in her tone.

"Lorenzo said he wanted to come back. I think something happened, but he hasn't told me what yet." Yvonne glanced at him.

"Who's on the phone at this time of the morning?" inquired a sleepy Lorenzo. He rolled over to place his arm across Yvonne's torso wrapping himself around her.

"It's your sister," she told him as she stroked his hair comfortingly.

That woke Lorenzo properly and he beckoned to Yvonne to hand the phone to him. The conversation was conducted in Italian.

"Maria, I brought Yvonne back to Glasgow last night because I wanted to get away from our father."

"Why would you do that?" she asked, sounding slightly hurt.

"When we were in his office after I proposed, we argued and he pulled out his gun. He pointed it at me, Maria. I know he wouldn't shoot me, but it felt like he might, and then Gio walked in on us."

There was a sharp inhalation at the other end of the phone. "Did that really happen Lorenzo?" her tone shocked and unbelieving.

"Yes. Why is that something I would make up?" he snapped back defensively.

"Does Yvonne know anything about this?"

"No, and I don't want her to know. I'm going to put her back on the phone now."

Her parting words were lost to an empty space as he handed the phone back to Yvonne.

"Hey Maria, please come over here soon. We still have to celebrate my engagement. I can't wait to have you as a sister-in-law!"

"Yes, I'll come over soon," Maria promised as the call ended. Lorenzo watched as she hung up the phone, before nuzzling into her neck.

"Do you honestly think I will let you out with my sister?" he asked, with a seductive undertone to his voice.

"Oh, I can be persuasive," she replied as she rolled her naked body over on top of his. They both sought comfort in each other.

"I think I'll take Italian lessons, so I know what you lot are speaking about when I'm around," announced Yvonne as she laid the table for breakfast. She was wearing one of Lorenzo's shirts, while he walked around in Armani boxer shorts. Their hair was messy and their hands wandering.

"I'll teach you the basics like yes, no, names and numbers," replied Lorenzo absentmindedly.

"Great, thank you, although I will end up needing more than that."

While the newly engaged couple were enjoying an extravagant breakfast together, Giovanni Maldini was clearing customs at Heathrow Airport. The thought of needing to take a transfer flight, as the jet had rudely been commandeered by Lorenzo, had aggravated his anger.

"There you go, sir, everything appears to be all in order." The immigration officer, handed back the passport and Giovanni looked up at the departures information board while making his way to buy a ticket to Glasgow.

"This weekend has been crazy, but strangely I loved it nearly as much as I love you, Lorenzo."

"Life in the Maldini family can be that way at times."

Lorenzo was still feeling guarded about his family, given what had happened in his father's office. He still had to tell Yvonne, but was waiting until he finished processing it himself.

"I better move and get back to my place. I have to be in the office early Tuesday morning and I have nothing to wear here."

"Let me know if you hear from my father." Lorenzo's request seemed to come from nowhere.

"Do you think he'll contact me again?"

"He can be persistent, you know. I'm sure he'll find a way to ask for what he wants."

She turned to leave, and as she was walking out the door, she called out "I love you," over her shoulder.

The door shut quietly behind her. Putting her travel bag into the car, Yvonne began the drive home in her new red Audi, reviewing everything that had gone on in Sardinia. As she was driving down Dumbarton Road towards her flat lost in her thoughts, she was startled by the phone ringing. The Bluetooth connection between her mobile and her car established automatically, and her left thumb touched the rocker switch on the steering wheel immediately connecting her to the caller. She recognised the voice immediately.

"Miss Duncan, Leonardo Maldini here."

"Hello again," she said politely.

"Miss Duncan, I wish to apologise for my son's behaviour in taking your beauty away from this island so suddenly." His voice was uncharacteristically smooth, and so she was wary.

"There's no need to apologise, Mr Maldini. He did what he thought was right."

"He is impulsive, as you will find out."

Yvonne did not have time for small talk. "Mr Maldini, why are you calling me?" she asked as she parked up outside of her building.

I must remember to register for a parking spot, everything's all been a bit of a whirlwind, she thought to herself.

"To make you an offer for your company, an offer you will not be able to refuse if you love my son."

"What does that mean?" Yvonne's eyes narrowing in suspicion as she cut the engine.

"I have instructed my nephew, Giovanni Maldini, to contact you. He lives in Glasgow too and I believe you may have been acquainted. He has a letter for you containing all the details of my offer, I think you should read it and consider it very carefully." The tone of his voice suggested there was no alternative option on offer.

Her voice turned steely as she challenged him. "Mr Maldini, are you threatening me? Maybe not the best thing to do, to be honest."

"No, absolutely not Miss Duncan. I'm just offering you some free business advice."

She knew that he was goading her and she was not going to rise to the bait. "Well sir, I don't need that from you, but thank you anyway. Goodbye." She ended the call.

Yvonne followed her usual security routine when she got into her flat. Bag on the floor and rooms checked. She was fuming. She shook off her jacket, throwing it over a nearby chair and stared at it as the compulsion to hang it neatly in its relegated spot overwhelmed her. Fulfilling her natural tidiness, she switched on the small light next to her settee and suddenly sensed that she was being watched. Without making it obvious, she glanced across the road to see the stranger watching her as she switched off the ceiling light. She recalled the conversation with Leonardo and considered all the aspects and realised, this must be cousin Giovanni.

She lifted her mobile telephone and called Lorenzo.

"Hi babe, is that you safely home?"

"Yes, thank you, but listen. There is something I have to tell you. Your father phoned me."

"When?" His tone was trying to be casual, but she could tell he was worried.

"When I was driving home."

"Why would he do that? He is such an idiot at times." He sounded increasingly annoyed.

"Lorenzo, I love you, but this could be the shortest engagement in history. Your father is trying to buy my company and is not taking no for an answer."

She heard silence from the other end of the phone. "Are you there Lorenzo?" Ensuring that she still had the opportunity to get her message across.

"Yes, sorry, yes I am here," he stammered, tripping over his words.

"Lorenzo, listen to me, if I find out you have anything to do with all this, anything at all, I will kill you."

"Yeah, right," he laughed, albeit nervously.

"Laugh all you like, but know that when I say something like that I am not joking." She was firm, she had to make sure he knew that she meant it.

"No, you aren't, are you?" He sighed.

"Why have you never introduced me to Giovanni?"

"We've been together a short time and I wanted to have you to myself. Why would I want to spend time with him?"

"Answer my question." She demanded again.

"Okay, okay. Actually, Gio hasn't been around, so that is why you haven't met him. Why are you asking?"

"Apparently, he has a letter for me from your father with an offer I 'cannot refuse'. How does he know where I am?"

"Well, you are all over the internet. Your company website has your details."

"Oh… I never thought of that, sorry," she said, slightly abashed. *Why didn't I think of that?* Yvonne was standing perfectly still as she maintained a calm tone, reassured that Lorenzo was not involved with his father's plot. Her shoulders relaxed as she began to plot.

"Listen, if Gio contacts you, call me immediately," he said, sounding concerned.

"Yes, sure thing. And before I forget, thank you for that whirlwind visit to your family. I love your sister, she is brilliant, and your mum too." Yvonne wanted to make sure that Lorenzo knew how much she appreciated and loved him before she turned against his father and his cousin.

"Yeah, they both are, but my father… we must build bridges with him, both of us. Together."

"I'll try, but it doesn't look great just now," she answered softly.

"Yvonne, I know this is the wrong thing to say about my father, I am his flesh and blood, but be careful please, I know what he can be like."

"What do you mean?" As before, her question was met by a long silence.

"He can make you a very rich lady, or he can break you and leave you with nothing," was his cryptic response.

"Do me a favour, please come over here right now." She demanded suddenly as an idea fell into place in her mind.

"Why?" It was Lorenzo's turn to be confused.

"I have a plan."

Chapter Thirteen

L orenzo arrived about thirty minutes later.

"Come in." Greeted Yvonne as she opened the door.

"What's this all about?" he asked as he squeezed past her into the hallway, noting that everything was in its place, as always.

They exited the narrow hallway into the living room. Yvonne ensured that they stayed as close to the door as possible, to avoid Giovanni spotting Lorenzo before she was ready.

"I've trusted you, now I need you to trust me." She held out her phone to him. "Give me your father's mobile number, please."

"Why?" he asked, bewildered. "I thought he called you?"

"It wasn't from his mobile, it may have been the house phone. I want to speak to him now and let's see how gutsy he really is."

"What do you mean, Yvonne?"

"Trust me."

Lorenzo searched his mobile for his father's number and transferred it into the phone that she held out to him. She took the phone back and placed a call to the newly created contact. The continental ringtone sounded in her ear.

"Ciao," came the greeting from the other end of the phone.

"Mr Maldini, this is Yvonne speaking." Her tone was self-confident, conveying that this was a business negotiation. "I wanted to let you know that I have spoken with Lorenzo. I am interested in what your offer is, but I am extremely busy today – I do have a company to run after all. However, Lorenzo has some time to spare so he will collect the letter from Giovanni."

She was met with silence. "Are you there, Mr Maldini?"

"Yes. Let me think, please, how we can arrange this."

"There is nothing to arrange. I have asked Lorenzo to collect the offer from his cousin in my place, and he has agreed. I'm merely calling you with this information as a courtesy."

"If you say so, Miss Duncan." The dial tone buzzed in her ear as he hung up abruptly.

Lorenzo had not moved throughout the duration of the phone call. He had simply waited, filling the doorway and listening intently to try and work out what was happening on the other end of the line. The next stage of Yvonne's plan was initiated as Yvonne moved into the middle of the living room. She knew that Lorenzo had a full view out of the window from his spot in the doorway and hoped that he would be hidden from the stranger's view.

"Now, I want you to tell me if you know this person. Can you see out of the window? Good. Don't move please."

She stared across the road, waiting. The only sound was the clock on the wall, ticking away as time marched on.

"What are you doing, Yvonne?" Lorenzo asked, his shoulders tense.

"Waiting on my perverted neighbour making an appearance."

"What do you mean?" He didn't have to wait long to find out, as a light came on in the flat opposite them.

"He loves watching me in here – now you watch this."

The stranger opposite stood staring into Yvonne's living room. He began to strip slowly, attempting to entice her to reciprocate. She did not participate

"Do you have any idea who he is, Lorenzo?"

"Yes," he said despairingly, as he looked out of the bay window. After a long pause, he sighed, "It's my cousin Giovanni."

At the revelation of this information, Yvonne turned away from Giovanni towards Lorenzo. With her suspicions confirmed, it was time to play her wild card. It was a big risk, but Leonardo had to know that she was not to be messed with.

"I think your cousin has been watching me on your father's instructions, and now he wants to blackmail me into selling my company. I'm going to put the ceiling light on, I want him to see you so that he knows I'm not backing down. Come and stand next to me."

As Yvonne lit up the room, Lorenzo joined her at her side, looking out at Giovanni. They presented themselves as a united front, and Yvonne fully expected Giovanni to pass along the development to Leonardo. Staring back, Giovanni knew he had been caught. He gathered his clothes back up and glared through the window as he turned the light off and left the room.

As the flat across the road plunged into darkness, Lorenzo turned to Yvonne to confront her.

"How he can blackmail you, Yvonne? What does he have on you? I need you to tell me," he pleaded.

As much as he was upset that there was some sordid affair between his fiancée and his cousin, he also loved her too much to let that get in the way. She took his hand and they sat down together on the settee.

"Lorenzo, before we got together, I was a single woman who enjoyed a bit of fun. You know that I wasn't a serial dater, so I settled for more…" Her brows furrowed as she searched for the right term. "…casual interludes. Your cousin was just another stranger to me. He moved in across the road only a couple of months ago. When I knew he was watching me, I had some fun stripping without closing the curtains. It was only fun, nothing else ever happened. I've never even spoken to him. To me, he was just someone who got his kicks by watching me and letting me watch him. Then he started following me around. That was a bit creepy, but somehow, I knew he wouldn't hurt me. Now I think he's been in your father's pocket all along, spying on me, which also makes me wonder how long my company has been a target."

"Did this continue after we got together?" Lorenzo was stone-faced.

"A couple of times, but not after things started to get serious between us."

Yvonne sat watching as Lorenzo tried to understand everything that she had just told him. She left him the same space that he had once left her during an argument, to show him how sincere she was and how much she loved him. She had done none of this to hurt him. He was motionless on his seat, and he could not look her in the eye. She was waiting for him to walk out.

"Okay," he said as he breathed out deeply, "we have to put this behind us. We have all done things we regret in the past and I'm no different." He paused briefly. "We are one, we are together, we will win this together."

She kissed him passionately, wrapping her arms around his neck. "Oh, Lorenzo! I'm so happy you are still here!"

He smiled as he kissed her back. "Shall we turn the lights off and have a little strip session of our own, then?" he suggested.

"I think we should," she purred in response.

Yvonne awoke to her phone ringing from her bedside table. As she answered, she heard, "Good morning, Miss Duncan."

"Good morning, Mr Maldini," she answered, putting her finger to her lips, signalling Lorenzo to be quiet and switching her mobile to the speaker. "What can I do for you?"

"Miss Duncan, Giovanni has explained to me what happened yesterday afternoon. What a mistake you have made."

"In what way?"

"You know exactly what I mean. So, today at three o'clock, Giovanni will arrive at your office with a revised offer for your company. My threat of telling Lorenzo your filthy little secret is no longer viable, so I am now going to deal with this bluntly."

Yvonne looked at Lorenzo, shaking her head and willing him to say nothing as his face turned crimson. "Out of interest, what was your original offer for my company?"

"Well, if you must know, it was one million euros, as you have created a little diamond in the publishing world. With me taking it to Europe and possibly worldwide, along with online sales, I thought that was more than a fair price. But it is too late for that now."

"What do you mean it was one million euros?" she asked as her eyes narrowed.

"Well, I was being generous. So, now it's only half a million, and I'll throw my idiot son into the deal."

"Tell Giovanni that I shall be waiting for him."

Lorenzo was gesturing wildly for the phone, his fury barely contained.

"Oh, hang on, please. Just one minute," Yvonne handed her mobile to Lorenzo, grinning.

The conversation immediately switched to Italian.

"Good morning. This is your 'idiot son' speaking. As of today, you are no longer my father. I don't know you, I have never met you, and before I go, tell Giovanni he is a dead man walking."

He hung up swiftly. He stared at the phone in his hand, as if in shock at the words that had just come out of his mouth, then quickly translated to Yvonne. She was shocked at his vehement attitude towards his father.

"Lorenzo, maybe we should call a halt to this. Me and you, go our separate ways. This was never meant to happen." Her voice trailed off into a whisper. "I don't want to get in the way of your family."

"Are you changing your mind from last night? Are you ending this?"

"No!" was her emphatic reply. "Absolutely not!"

"Right, that's it then. It's you and me from here on out."

Lorenzo's phone then burst into life with a text message;

*hai finito, non, sei più mio figlio, l'hai scelta sulla
tua famiglia.*

He read it silently, then translated it out loud. "'You're done, you're not my son anymore, you chose her over your family'."

"Lorenzo!" exclaimed Yvonne, looking aghast.

He sat staring at the message forlornly. "If we're together, I will be okay," he answered firmly, aware of the significance of his choice.

He reached over for her hand and held onto it like he was drowning. His face showed no emotion.

"Yes, Lorenzo I promise, we will be. Honey, I have to go to work, but I'll check in with you this afternoon. Everything's going to be okay." Yvonne wanted to reassure him as she kissed the top of his head.

Once in her car, she made a telephone call.

"Yvonne. What do you want now?" said Leonardo with a sigh

"Me, Giovanni and your offer. Tell him to meet me on the west side of the River Clyde, opposite Cessnock Festival Park at three-thirty this afternoon where I will be waiting for him. Alone."

"I do not understand. Can I ask why?"

"Yes, certainly you can ask." She paused for a few seconds before explaining herself, "I'd like to see your offer in writing, and also to say goodbye to him. I fully expect our business to be concluded after this meeting."

"What does that mean?"

"Just tell him to be there."

After a long pause he cut off the call.

"Good morning," Yvonne's usual greeting sang through the air as she strode into the office. She hung her leather jacket up on the sleek silver coat stand that waited in her office, before going back into the main space. She paused at her assistant's desk which was once again occupied.

"Hi, Anne. I didn't know you'd be coming back in today. How are you?"

Anne looked up from her computer where she was already powering through the backlog of emails that had accumulated during her absence.

"Hi, Yvonne. I'm okay. I enjoyed having a bit of time with Mum to adjust, but I'm so happy to be back at work to have something else to think about."

"That's great to hear. Remember I'm here for you and if you need more time off, don't hesitate to take it." Yvonne gave her assistant's shoulder a reassuring squeeze before addressing the rest of the office.

"Okay everyone, stop for a moment please." Work came to a grinding halt. "Everyone put your phones on silent please, ignore landline calls. For the last few days, I have been in Sardinia—"

"Alright for some," muttered Gordon.

"Gordon, will you please refrain from interrupting?"

"Yes Yvonne," he replied sheepishly.

"Right, hush then," she admonished insincerely. He had been her friend and confidant of many years, and this was standard practice for them.

"I shall begin again, if Gordon can stay silent. Over the past weekend, I was in Sardinia where I met the Maldini family. Now, before the rumours start, I will confirm that I'm dating Lorenzo Maldini. He manages gyms across Scotland on behalf of his father who owns a variety of businesses including a successful winery.

Yvonne paused to gauge their reactions, then continued. "Yesterday, Leonardo Maldini offered me one million euros for this company."

"You are joking?" gasped Gordon in disbelief.

"No, but due to... due to... let's just say this. He's a lowlife who is trying to screw me. I intend on digging in my Scottish heels and tell him to stick his euros where the sun will never see it!"

Her speech elicited audible gasps from her staff. She was always so proper, so professional, but this situation was draining, and it felt good to be blunt.

"Why?" asked Gordon.

"Because he thinks I'm soft and I will just capitulate in the face of his massive wealth which I absolutely will not."

"So, what are you going to do?"

"What am I going to do? I'm going to show him that he cannot push me around. Specifically this afternoon. Now, as for you all, and where you are in all of this. We've been together since the beginning, some a little more than others, but not by much. If I do decide to sell out, I will share it all with you and that is my promise." She took a deep breath as she finished her speech, hoping it had reassured them, wondering if it had been the right thing to tell them about the potential sale.

"Now, I have to go out so anything you have for me, tell me now."

"Yvonne, may I ask something?" ventured Anne, raising her hand slightly, as if she were in school and talking to a teacher.

"Sure."

"What is that giant rock on your left hand?" She pointed and all of the staff followed her finger to the ring on Yvonne's hand.

"Oh, I forgot to mention. I am engaged."

She could not help the grin that spread across her face as she flashed off her favourite new accessory. Calls of congratulations reverberated from her staff happily as they returned to their desks. Yvonne entered her office and locked the door.

At precisely two o'clock, Yvonne left the office giving her time to get home and changed. For this particular meeting, she had donned a long blonde wig, her favourite calf-length, vixen leather coat which covered a scarlet blouse, and tight leather trousers. Her sturdy, yet fashionable, knee-length black leather boots completed the outfit. Staring at herself in the mirror, she admired the transformation.

She drove to the River Clyde and parked in a nearby hotel car park and walked along the pathway, glancing across to the building which housed the television stations and the Children's Science Centre which was specifically focused on enhancing children's interest in science. A quick view assured her there was not a camera in sight, so nothing would show she was or had ever been, in the area.

"Miss Duncan." The strong New York accent emitted from the shadow of the car park. Giovanni pushed off the wall where he had been reclining, flicking a cigarette butt to the ground.

"So, what do you have for me, big boy?" drawled Yvonne seductively.

Moving closer to Giovanni as he strode towards her, closing the gap between them, she was fully embracing her inner vixen as she slipped her hand between his legs. Giovanni stared at her through narrowed eyes, suspicious of her motives. She could tell he enjoyed being close to her. He handed her the envelope from Leonardo which she put into an inside pocket of her coat. Glancing around furtively, Yvonne confirmed that it was only Giovanni and herself along the length of the quayside pathway. She put her hand around the back of his neck and pulled him in closer. Gazing into his eyes, their lips met, and he wrapped his arms around her. They kissed passionately. Without breaking apart, she reached into her pocket and taking a locking knife in her right hand she released the blade which plunged deeply into Giovanni's stomach. She then pulled upwards, practically disembowelling him on the spot, only stopping their kiss as he sank to his knees and collapsed onto the ground. His body leaned to the left and the retaining barrier along the pathway failed to stop him from rolling off the path. Yvonne watched as his body sank into the river, deep and out of sight. The water was too murky to show the blood draining from his body. She looked at the knife in her gloved hand, covered in blood, and dropped it to the ground. With a flick of her foot, the murder weapon followed the victim.

Yvonne strolled along the quayside back towards her car like any casual tourist. Joggers and cyclists, businesspeople finished at work for the day, teenagers not ready to go home from school yet – they all began to pass by, unaware of what had happened only moments before. There was nothing that she could do about the blood on the pathway, and she knew that it would not be long before the alarm was raised.

Chapter Fourteen

Yvonne was in her car driving home when her phone began to ring, through the car.

"Hello?"

"Yvonne," answered Lorenzo.

"Hi, honey."

"I've been phoning you for ages. Where have you been?"

"Yes, sorry. I was in a business meeting, I was just about to call you back." She lied casually. Glancing down she noticed some small blood droplets across the front of her coat and she was thankful for her choice of a red chiffon blouse.

Can't take this to the dry cleaners, she thought drily.

"Did you see Giovanni?"

"Yes." She wanted to keep whatever Lorenzo knew to a minimum in case her plan went awry, so she decided to keep her answers short.

"Did he deliver the envelope?"

"Yes."

"Where did you meet him?" Lorenzo was fishing for information, and she had to give him something, or he would be suspicious.

"At the bottom of Buchanan Street."

"Good I'm glad about that; he can be a crazy dude if you'd met him elsewhere. I'm glad you're okay," he exhaled, genuinely relieved.

"Honestly, I'm fine Lorenzo." She paused. "Would you like to come and stay at mine tonight? Have a few drinks and see what happens?"

"Yvonne, you can be so bad when you want to be," he laughed.

"Oh, I know that. See you later." She hung up as she pulled into a public car wash to remove any evidence that she may have left on the door handles or bodywork.

While the sudsy water poured over the car, she reviewed the scene in meticulous detail. Nothing would have her fingerprints, the knife was 'borrowed' from a friend years ago. The ruined coat and bloody gloves were in a plastic bag and the boots would have to join them before she destroyed all the evidence.

A short time later she arrived home, undressed and immediately placed all her remaining clothing into yet another plastic bag, and then stepped into a hot, steamy shower. As she stood there with the water pouring over her body and steam slowly filling the room, she closed her eyes, the events of the day unfolding before her like a film. A little thrill ran down her spine as she recalled the adrenaline rush of killing Giovanni.

She eventually stepped out from the shower and wrapped herself in a plush white towel before walking into the living room. Stopping to look across the road at the darkened living room that had once been occupied by Giovanni, a sense of intense pleasure shot through her body, more intense than the one from the shower. She sat down, closing her eyes to embrace the feeling before she was interrupted by a loud, sudden knock that startled her from her reverie. She rose from her seat, her heart racing, peering through the little spy hole set into the door. Once she saw who it was, she reached up to unlock the door.

"Come in," she purred.

Loosening the towel she returned to the living room and let it drop to the floor. She was glistening as water droplets on her shoulders caught the light, and she knew he could not resist her.

"You're early," she whispered into Lorenzo's ear, wrapping her arms around his neck and kissing him fiercely as he dragged his fingernails gently up her back, causing her to draw him in closer. He was less gentle as she felt his hands take hold of her buttocks, squeezing them tightly and pulling her in towards his groin. There was an urgency to their desire. Their lips separated as they gazed into each other's eyes. She stripped him naked then pushed him down onto the floor before straddling him. As she made love to Lorenzo, she envisioned the knife going into

Giovanni's body, his stomach being opened like a ripe tomato, his warm blood running onto her hand as she pulled the knife upwards, watching as he collapsed at her feet, his body rolling into the River Clyde. Her breath quickened with her movements and Lorenzo matched her speed underneath. In slow motion, she watched as her knife fell onto the pathway, her foot flicking it into the river as she collapsed onto her lover, breathing heavily.

"Wow. Oh my god. I don't know what you've been doing today or what's got you so excited but wow… whatever it is, keep it up because that was awesome." He was panting, little beads of sweat covering his forehead. He held her close.

"Really? Whatever it was, you want me to do it again?" she asked slyly.

"Oh, hell yes. If this is the result, definitely." He kissed her deeply, ecstatic about the experience they had just shared. "So, are you gonna tell me what brought this surge of passion on?"

Yvonne leaned forward, still straddled on top of him and whispered into his ear, "Baby, you don't want to know," as she nibbled his earlobe, before slipping off him and lying on her side, placing her arm across his body as she tightly snuggled into him. She was still wet, except now with sweat.

"Tell me something," Yvonne said as she ran her finger down his torso towards his navel and back up again, slowly and continuously. She took a deep breath. "If you love me as much as I love you, what's the most outrageous thing that you would do for me?"

"That's one hell of a question, Yvonne and I want to reverse it. What's the most outrageous thing you would do for me?"

Yvonne lay silent for a moment, continuing to run her finger over his torso, "I would kill for you," she whispered, before placing her hand flat on his chest. The sudden stillness hung over them heavily. They lay like that on the living room floor for a few moments before going into the bedroom.

The orange glow of the sodium streetlights shone through the bedroom window overlooking Dumbarton Road in the early evening darkness. Buses and cars passed the flat with monotonous regularity, headlights blazing, briefly illuminating the bedroom, and overpowering the streetlights. The white noise was pleasant.

Lorenzo lay on his back staring at the ceiling in silence. His right arm was under Yvonne's head, his fingers slowly and gently massaging her arm as she lay beside him, the only noise was the sound of their breathing. As he turned towards her, his left arm went over her body, as if protecting her.

"I have to ask you something."

"Sure, anything."

"You know that I love you like nobody before."

"If you say so," was her cheeky reply. There was, however, no depth to her response as they were both exhausted.

"I do say so! And it's a fantastic feeling," his tone gentle like a caress.

"I feel the same." Yvonne nuzzled into him, placing her head in the space between his neck and his shoulder.

"You know how you picked up the envelope from Gio today?"

"Yes."

"You don't have to answer this if you don't want to... but what was in it?"

He pulled away slightly to look at her face. He caught a flash of annoyance before her features smoothed over into a reassuring gaze.

"It was an offer for my company."

"The same as the one he made on the phone?" he inquired.

"Yep."

"And what reply are you sending to him, via Gio, of course."

"Oh, that's easy. Two words, nothing more. As a lady, the first word begins with 'F' and the second word is off. I have no interest in giving up my company," she replied.

"Short and sharp then?" Lorenzo laughed and kissed the top of her head.

"Yes, I suppose so" she replied, leaning into him. "Do you know something? I would like to see your sister again, even if I've pissed off your dad. She was so much fun!"

"Okay, I'll call her and ask, babe. Now, is there any chance of something to eat? I'm starving after that."

Chapter Fifteen

The radio alarm went off at seven in the morning, waking both Yvonne and Lorenzo who were still wrapped in each other's arms. They kissed fervently, pressing against each other as they explored every inch of their bodies, the duvet became entangled between them as they moved closer together.

They were interrupted by a tinny voice from the bedside radio announcing: *this is the seven-thirty news.*

Yvonne's heart erupted out of her chest. She had been on edge since the day before, seeking solace in Lorenzo. Three minutes later, Yvonne breathed a huge sigh of relief when there was no mention of Giovanni before the programme went into its morning chat show.

"You okay?" asked Lorenzo as he turned his attention back to Yvonne, trailing his hand up her thigh.

"Oh yes, I'm fine. Stay there, I'll be back."

Yvonne rose from the bed and left the room. She grabbed her silk kimono dressing gown from the back of the door on her way out, cinching it tightly around her waist. The unwelcome interruption of the news report created butterflies in her stomach, something not even Lorenzo could dissipate, and she did want him to notice anything *off* about her.

As Lorenzo lay on the bed, the smell of bacon and eggs frying in the kitchen began to waft into the bedroom.

"Yvonne, hurry up with that!" he shouted.

Suddenly ravenous his stomach rumbled to help prove his point. As a personal trainer, he had a passion for fitness and the two of them had worked out a lot last night. A short time later she returned to the room, carefully balancing a tray with two mugs of coffee and a single plate filled with a wonderful selection of bacon, eggs, sausage, black pudding and potato scones, the smell of fried food causing Lorenzo's stomach to growl even louder as it demanded to be fed.

"To keep my lover fit for action," she laughed, planting a kiss on his cheek as she presented the tray.

"To get your lover's cholesterol sky high, you mean," he remarked in jest as he eyed the plate.

"Are you hungry or not? And no, I don't have time to eat before I leave for work."

"Bloody starving, although I loved last night's snack." His cheeky remark was accompanied by an equally cheeky grin.

"Me too," she answered just as cheekily. "When's your first client?" she asked as she crawled back into bed beside him.

"Midday," he mumbled around a mouthful of food. He happily tucked into his plate despite his earlier grumblings.

"Right, we have to get you and Gordon together and sort out your book. I'm leaving shortly, and you need to be at the office no later than ten."

"Eh?" He looked up with his cheeks full. He resembled a hamster and Yvonne's heart skipped a beat at just how precious he was.

"You heard me, no later than ten," she repeated as she left the bed for the second time, downing the final sip of her coffee.

She was now in business mode, the caffeine stimulating all of her nerves, increasing her energy for the day.

"Oh, and wash the plates before you leave please."

Half an hour later, showered and dressed, Yvonne was out of the house and heading for the office. It was rush hour as everyone fought to get to work on time, which was much more difficult in a car than on the public transport that Yvonne was used to travelling in. She kept her eyes on the road, paying attention to who was out at this time. Police cars sat outside cafes as officers grabbed greasy breakfasts, ambulances with blaring sirens cut through the morning air. Being a murderer made you pay attention to the authorities, and Yvonne noticed that the roads were starting to get busy.

"Morning gang. Meeting time."

Yvonne headed directly into her office to deposit her coat before gathering the necessary materials for the morning debrief in the conference room.

"I take it Lorenzo stayed over," gossiped Gordon to some of the other staff quietly... well, almost quietly.

"Gordon, you have a whisper like the roar of a lion," admonished Yvonne sternly.

She did not appreciate people discussing her private life behind her back. Her staff knew this and there was an embarrassed shuffling of feet as everyone got settled into the conference room, unwilling to push their boss further.

"So what do we have today?"

Each member of staff went through their tasks for the day.

When Gordon began to speak Yvonne interrupted. "What you have is Lorenzo coming in at about ten. Confirm the work completed so far on his fitness book and then start the timeline. Also, I want a video session arranged to accompany the release of the book. Show me a schedule by the end of the day and we will get dates approved."

"And what about the rest of my appointments?"

"Gordon, do you have anything at that time of the morning?"

"No..." he replied sullenly.

"Right, so what is the problem?"

"Nothing, Yvonne."

"Good," she stated, effectively ending the meeting.

About ten o'clock Lorenzo walked into the office in his tracksuit and greeted promptly by Gordon, who pulled in a spare desk chair for Lorenzo to work at the cramped desk,.

"First, I want you to run me through our – I mean your – specific fitness programmes. We have to arrange a photoshoot and a video to accompany the release of the book, so it would be good to know what will be included, then I will start writing based on what you show me today."

"Simple as that?" Lorenzo's eyebrows raised with his question.

"For now."

Yvonne watched the interaction between Gordon and Lorenzo through the glass panels of her office. She knew Gordon was on his game, noting the details while making telephone calls, probably arranging the videographer and photographer. Lorenzo demonstrated a few exercises that would be included in the final product. She decided to head over and find out how it was progressing.

"Hi." Yvonne placed her hand on Lorenzo's shoulder. "How are things going over here?"

"Hey. You startled me." Lorenzo kissed the back of her hand affectionately.

"Good," replied Gordon, "It's slow-going but we are getting a picture of how this project will pan out. He's not a best-selling author yet, but I think we'll get there. Actually, Yvonne, before I forget, just to confirm the name of the book that these expenses will go against?"

"Create one for Lorenzo Maldini Fitness Guru as a working title please, until we finalise the title."

She walked briskly back to her office, beckoned by the ringing telephone.

"What does that mean?" asked a bewildered Lorenzo.

"Means that any work that is done is billed to the correct title to keep the bookkeeper happy," laughed Gordon, his computer keys clacking as he swiftly created an account for the new book with Lorenzo's details.

"I don't believe her, she's something else," laughed Lorenzo, watching Yvonne lovingly who was gesturing animatedly around her as she spoke on the phone in her office.

"Well, that's how she's got to where she is today. You don't mess with Yvonne. Oh, and another thing as far as she's concerned. While you're sitting here, working on a project for her company, you are a Yvonne Duncan Publications client, nothing more," he explained, staring Lorenzo straight in the eye, almost willing him to be defiant. "Now, back to work."

An hour later, the basic layout for the book was finished and appointments for relevant photo shoots and video sessions were scheduled. Lorenzo's diary was scribbled in and fully booked by the time he stood up and shook hands with Gordon before sneaking into Yvonne's office.

"Hey, my place when you finish. Just go straight there. I'll get there around nine as I have some business in the gym once clients are done for the day but make yourself at home."

"Sure, see you later," she replied as she flashed the keycard at him so that he knew she would get in.

Just before eight o'clock, Yvonne arrived at Lorenzo's. She pulled smoothly into the private parking area before heading up to his floor. For all the times she had been in this building, there was never another soul in the corridors. She wondered grimly if Leonardo Maldini owned the whole building – it would not surprise her. As she approached the door, she noticed that the lights were on in his apartment, sneaking through the gap between the door and the floor. She hadn't expected him to be home until later. He must have finished everything at the gym quicker than he planned.

"Hi honey," she shouted as she entered the apartment. She was met by an eerie silence. An ominous, oppressive silence. Withdrawing her key-card from the lock, her eyes slowly scanned the hallway. Yvonne began to feel uneasy and as the door closed behind her she slowly moved through the apartment. Her previous trauma of being robbed was flashing through her head. Heart pounding, palms sweating, and there was an ever-increasing buzz in her ears as her panic increased. Something in her head said this idiot is going to jump out from somewhere for a laugh.

"Lorenzo?" she cried out but again there was no reply. She went into the kitchen and opened a drawer, quietly lifting a large-bladed knife, which caught the light as she inspected it and she glimpsed her reflection in it. Her skin was pale and sweaty, but her expression was firm and defiant as the vixen-survivor personality came to her rescue. She was ready to defend herself as she hid the knife behind her back with the blade pointing upwards, perfectly positioned to strike. With her left hand, she opened the living room door, the pounding in her ears matching the rapid beating of her heart, where she saw the reflection of a man facing the street in the large living room window.

"Good evening, Miss Duncan."

Leonardo Maldini refused to turn around. He stood straight his hands clasped behind his back. He was wearing a dark blue tailored suit and a chunky gold ring adorned one of his fingers. The symbol on it was unrecognisable, yet it had a strange familiarity. She felt she should know this signet ring of an unremembered organisation.

"What the hell are you doing here?" Her quiet yet malicious tone dripping with venom.

Her previously shaky hand settled as she assessed the situation, more confident in now knowing her opponent.

"I go where I want when I want, and I am here to see my son," he replied, shrugging his shoulders.

Leonardo finally turned away from the window to face her as he walked over to one of the chairs that sat opposite the settee and settled into it. Then leaning forward authoritatively his fingers raised into a steeple, like a church spire, tapping together as he stared at Yvonne. It was the only sound in the room as they stared each other down. The tension heavy and cloying.

"Sit Miss Duncan, please, and put that knife down before you hurt yourself." He pointed to her right hand as she sat precariously on the edge of the settee, poised to run should she need to. She glared at Leonardo, the knife lying on the seat beside her, but within reach, if needed. There was an eerie silence that seemed to stretch on forever.

"Miss Duncan, I spoke to Lorenzo today, and he does not yet know that I am here. Let's say, this will be a surprise for him when he gets home. You and me together. What will he think? I am expecting him here at nine o'clock, but our business will be concluded before then. I would like to explain to you what will happen. I am prepared to offer you one-point-five million euros for your company. I am going to give you the contract and as each minute goes by that you do not accept my offer, it will reduce by one-hundred-thousand euros."

Yvonne's eyes narrowed as he continued speaking and her lips tightened. Her breathing pattern signalled anger and she used deep breaths to calm her nerves.

"You don't look pleased Miss Duncan. What are you going to do, take me to the river and dispose of me as you did with Giovanni?"

Leonardo smirked, although it did not reach his eyes. His fingers continued to tap out an ominous beat breaking the silence. If this were a game of poker, then Leonardo held a full house. Nothing was said as they continued to stare at each other. Leonardo checked the ornate watch that adorned his wrist.

"Five minutes dear lady," he announced, pushing an envelope across the table towards her.

She stared at it as he checked his watch again. "Four minutes, Miss Duncan, and counting."

He clasped his hands behind his head as he leaned back in the chair.

Yvonne rose from the couch, tearing the envelope open. Inside was a legal contract giving her one-point-five-million euros in exchange for one hundred percent of her shares in her company. Leonardo Maldini would be the sole owner while she would be reduced to nothing, but she would have her freedom from a life sentence for the murder of Giovanni.

"Miss Duncan, you have just over a minute to decide," he reminded her as he picked up his mobile telephone. "I believe the number for the police in this country is 999?" His thumb hovered threateningly over the buttons.

Yvonne signed on the dotted line.

"Thank you, Yvonne. That was a wise decision," he said as he signed his name next to hers.

He then arranged for a mobile transfer of the money from his Swiss bank account to hers. "Now, may we go to where you murdered my nephew, so I may pay my last respects?"

"He was a disposable asset" she replied casually. Yvonne's mobile vibrated loudly in the heavy silence between them.

"What is that noise?"

She checked her phone. "Bank notification."

"I suggest you check it then."

Yvonne keyed in her password and she watched the text message confirmation appear on her screen. *One-point-five-million euros transferred in full. LM.*

She logged into her bank account. Every cent was there.

"Happy?" he asked.

"Mess with me and you will be seeing Giovanni in the afterlife sooner than you think."

"Surely I have proven that I am trustworthy? You have the money. Now, please take me to Gio, for the last time."

Chapter Sixteen

After a few tumultuous weeks, where she had been anything but on time, Yvonne turned the key to her office and noticed she was the first in. Surveying the desks and the chairs belonging to her four staff members it was Gordon's desk that she cherished most, as he had been there from the very beginning. He was the one who had faith in her in those early days and she could not help the slight smile that played around the corner of her lips as she thought of their fond memories together. He had been there through the thick and thin of starting a company and despite other offers he had stuck by Yvonne. She laid an envelope on Gordon's desk, as she did with the other three, with the words 'Thank You' on the front. Yvonne watched from her office as her staff arrived for work, trickling in one by one. Gordon was last in.

"What's up?" he asked looking at the envelopes in their hands.

He put down his shoulder bag and hung up his jacket. No one said a word. As he sat at his desk, he noticed an identical envelope lay before him, he picked it up and sliced it with the letter opener that Yvonne had given him as a present years before. Pulling out the contents, he read the attached letter:

> *For all the years and everything that we have been*
> *through together, through the good and the bad,*
> *you have been a fantastic colleague and a true friend.*
> *With love,*
> *Yvonne x*

Attached was a company cheque in his name for one-hundred-thousand pounds.

Gordon studied the cheque, gobsmacked at the absurdity of the situation, before looking into Yvonne's office. He placed the letter back into the envelope, before rising from his chair and walking over to her door.

"Come in," she called, knowing what was about to come. Gordon sat down facing Yvonne, his hands clasped together and resting on his lap.

"Well?" she asked after a minute passed in silence. "You haven't come over here to just sit there and say nothing," she snapped, going on the defensive. The pitch of her voice rose ever so slightly, which was the only indication that she was stressed about the situation. "Spit it out."

"So, you sold your soul to the devil," Gordon said solemnly, pausing as he looked down at his thumbs pressed against each other.

"Gordon, I received an offer that I could not refuse. I've shared some of that with you and the girls so that life for you all could be more comfortable. How long would it have taken you to earn that?"

Gordon did not acknowledge what she was saying as he sat staring at his clasped hands. Another minute passed. "I've been doing a bit of research on the Maldini family."

Yvonne felt her heart skip a beat. "Have you been spying on Lorenzo?" There is no way he could know everything that has happened.

"No," he replied quickly, "I've been reading about the family in general."

"And?"

"His father is connected."

"Gordon, speak in an everyday language please," sighed Yvonne. She was exasperated by his uninformative tidbits of information, and she did not attempt to hide it.

"Do you remember way back when you got with Lorenzo, I joked about the Mafia?"

Yvonne nodded quickly, her lips clamped tight, and her eyebrows furrowed.

"Well, it appears that I was not that far out of line. Yvonne, go online and search *Maldini family* and *Italy*."

Gordon sat and watched her closely as she stared at the screen her eyes rapidly swinging from left to right as she scanned the contents on the Maldini family. As she clicked link after link, each story detailing how Leonardo accumulated his wealth by destroying others was the same.

"Right," she announced, switching off her desktop monitor, "let's go."

"Let's go where?" He was left unanswered as she swept out into the main office and made a general announcement.

"Close the office. We're off on a little outing."

"To where?" asked Anne, eyes darting around the room as everyone wondered what was going on.

"To the bank," stated Yvonne.

After the staff of Yvonne Duncan Publications had arrived and asked for an appointment, a banking assistant sidled up to Yvonne nervously.

"Miss Duncan, hello. I believe our manager wants to see you."

"Yes, I am sure he does. However, I have more pressing matters, so take us to a private room please. I'll book an appointment with him next week."

Yvonne's tone left no room for argument and so the assistant ran off abashed. The group waited in the entrance until Yvonne was called into a little private room off to the right.

"How can I help you?" asked the bank clerk.

"I want to transfer some money, so please bring up my account."

Yvonne sat on the uncomfortable chair with her legs and arms crossed, presenting herself as the definition of authority. Her fiery red hair was swept back into a business ponytail, and she was about to make some major decisions.

So each member of Yvonne's team would have privacy, they were called in one by one to join Yvonne until it was only Gordon left. Anne came out of the room looking astounded, her eyes glazed over. Gordon guided her to a chair to recover, then entered the room himself, uneasy about what was going to happen. He sat next to Yvonne, and she smiled at him.

"How much to this account, Miss Duncan?" asked the clerk for the final time.

Yvonne turned to face him. "Gordon, how much is left on your mortgage?"

"What?"

"You heard me. How much is left on your mortgage?"

"About eighty-five-thousand pounds."

Yvonne looked pointedly at the clerk, who had performed this action three times already. "Transfer one-hundred-and-twenty-five-thousand pounds, please."

The blood drained from his face. He felt faint and stammered "Yvonne, w-, what the f—"

"Gordon, shut up," she interrupted, not allowing him to finish his sentence.

"Is that everything, Miss Duncan?" asked the bank clerk, authorising the transaction.

"Yes, thank you."

They stood up to leave, passing by the bank manager who had come to speak to Yvonne. She smiled at him charmingly but gave him no opportunity to say anything before she had breezed out of the building, followed by her bewildered entourage.

As they crowded into Yvonne's parked car, there was a sense of camaraderie and achievement. None of the employees knew where the money had come from – bar Gordon – but they were too giddy to question it.

"What now, Yvonne?" asked Gordon.

"Well, if the girls agree, we stick together like the five musketeers."

"I thought it was the three musketeers?" asked Anne.

"Actually, there were four musketeers Anne, but the point is that there are five of us!"

"More important what does that mean?" Gordon was determined to find out what Yvonne was thinking.

Yvonne sat staring out of the windscreen of her car contemplating her answer, her hands wrapped around the steering wheel firmly, leaning forward, lost in her thoughts, while formulating her plan of action.

"I'll tell you what it means. I am going to call all of our clients and ask them to move to a new company, leaving the new owner of Yvonne Duncan Publications with an empty shell. How does Yvonne Duncan and Company sound to you all?"

"We're in!" Was the enthusiastic chorus of all the women.

"Gordon, you're very quiet," Yvonne prompted, looking at him sitting next to her. "Gordon?"

He turned and looked at Yvonne and said with a deep sigh, "One for all and all that musketeer stuff. Let's do it."

He grinned apprehensively, attempting to appear more jovial than he felt.

"Great, back to the office, and let's hit the phones."

Yvonne was not unmindful to his unease, but she was not going to press him in front of their oblivious colleagues who were animatedly chattering away in the back of the car.

With the speed of a demon, Yvonne activated Yvonne Duncan and Company – a name she had registered years before and kept alive just in case. As someone with foresight and one who tended to be more paranoid than not, she had felt a backup domain was necessary for any mishaps. She was glad of her foresight now.

By nine o'clock that night, those clients who could be reached were on board with the new company and only a few of the minor authors were left to be contacted and new contracts would follow the next day for a smooth transition. As Yvonne brought a bottle of champagne into the main office to celebrate, she offered a toast.

"You guys are the company. Here is to Yvonne Duncan and Company, now active in 2021."

They chatted and laughed and eventually, as the evening came to an end, leaving Gordon and Yvonne alone in the office.

"So, Gordon, when your wife goes to the cash dispenser tomorrow and sees all that dosh in your account, what are you going to say?"

"I'll tell her the truth, Yvonne."

"And what is the truth?"

"One hard-nosed bitch of a business lady from Glasgow screwed the Italian Mafia." He raised his glass to her.

"She won't believe you, Gordon." Yvonne laughed as she laid her empty glass on his desk.

"Yeah, that's the sad thing," he replied. The smile on his lips did not reach his eyes and she wondered what he was thinking. "Maybe we should write a book about it."

She didn't pry. Instead, she simply said, "Lock up on your way out. And thank you for sticking with me."

"Sure thing, Yvonne, sure thing," murmured Gordon, as he watched her heading out the door.

As Yvonne prepared for her journey home, she had a feeling that she was being watched. She stood with her back against the car, her eyes panning around for the slightest sign of life, she became more tense and alert. Yvonne slipped her right hand into her pocket where she kept a locking knife – identical to the one that had disposed of Giovanni. With a flick of her thumb, the blade was released, awaiting a victim. It was almost distressing how quickly she had become accustomed to the idea of murder. *It's really only self-defence if you think about it*, she attempted to justify to herself.

"Miss Duncan," emerged a deep, gravelly, disembodied voice from the darkness in the car park. "Your days are numbered."

The air around Yvonne dropped a couple of degrees, and it was uncharacteristically still.

"Meaning what?" Her eyes darted around trying to trace the location of the voice.

"Do not move, Miss Duncan. Get into your vehicle and go home. Have a good evening."

She fumbled with the door handle and sped away as soon as she started the engine. Every action seemed to take an eternity as fear overwhelmed her. It was one thing being ready to defend yourself against someone you could see but being threatened by the overarching darkness was an unparalleled fear.

By the time she reached her flat she was wracked with anxiety. It took several attempts to get the key into the lock, her hand was shaking so much that she did not have the strength to turn it when she eventually did manage to get it in. Once she finally opened the door, she almost collapsed into her flat and immediately locked the door securely behind her. She pulled the locking knife from her pocket, the blade drawn as she went around the flat room by room on high alert. Once she had inspected every inch of her flat, she sank into the settee in the living room, which was bathed in familiar orange sodium light from the street, the knife still gripped firmly in her hand. It was only at that moment that her heart began to slow, and she felt that she could take a proper breath. She rested her head on the back of the seat and closed her eyes, exhausted as the adrenaline flooded from her body. Her phone rang with Lorenzo's designated ringtone, causing her to wake abruptly.

"Hello?"

Silence.

"Hello?" she repeated. She could make out muffled breathing but received no answer.

"Lorenzo, speak to me." When she was once again left unanswered, she hung up and called Lorenzo's office number immediately.

He picked up after one ring. "Hiya, you okay?" He paused while he waited for her to answer.

She struggled to speak, her body shaking with newfound terror. "Yeah, I'm okay, but could you come over here please? I need you."

"Sure, can you give me an hour?"

"Yes but call me when you get here so I know that it's you at the door?"

"Sure," he said, "see you soon. I love you."

Yvonne poured herself a glass of chilled white wine and sat down. Then the light in Giovanni's flat flicked on unexpectedly. A shiver of cold, concentrated anxiety drove down her spine as she stared out across the road. Wearing a leather coat, leather trousers and gloves, the whole ensemble topped off with a Stetson hat, someone stood in the centre of the living room. She knew it could not be Giovanni, no, this was a different stranger. As her breathing got heavier and time slowed, she watched as the person slowly lifted their gaze from the floor, raising their arms and pointing a handgun towards her. She sat motionless, rooted to the seat in fear, as her mobile telephone rang into life beside her. Shaken from her paralysis, she jumped to answer it and ducked under the window to protect herself.

"Lorenzo, get up here!" she screamed down the phone

"I'm outside your door."

She crawled across the floor into the hallway, keeping low and out of sight. She opened the door and returned to the living room, dragging Lorenzo towards the ground. Fear flashed across his face as she started gesturing to Giovanni's flat.

"Look, look across the road Lorenzo," she babbled nervously, pointing over to the flat opposite.

"What am I looking for?" he asked as he crouched behind her.

"Someone holding the gun! Do you not see?" She was frantic, and she needed him to see it.

"Yvonne, the flat is in darkness, look."

"No, no, no, someone was there, Lorenzo."

He wrapped his arms tightly around her.

"What is going on Yvonne?"

Her muscles were tense and ready to run, then she began to relax in his warm and loving embrace. Her breathing slowed. She took a deep breath, collecting her thoughts.

"I don't know. Someone came to the office car park and told me my days were numbered."

"Who was it?" His tone had a nervous edge.

"I don't know. He stood in the darkness and told me not to turn around."

"Okay, sit down, let's get you a cup of tea," he said soothingly, trying to calm her.

As Lorenzo hurried to the kitchen, his mobile telephone rang.

"Maria. How are you, sister?" was all that Yvonne understood as the conversation continued in Italian.

The call ended after about ten minutes, and Lorenzo entered the living room with a concerned look on his face.

"Is everything okay?" she asked, reaching for him. She desperately needed his physical reassurance while she was still recovering from the shock of the evening's events.

"Maria was asking if our father was here in Glasgow," he replied, tapping his phone on his chin in thought.

"Why would she think he was here?"

"Because his jet is at Glasgow airport."

"Oh, but there is nothing to say that he is the one came over here. Is there?"

Yvonne remembered the conversation in Lorenzo's flat and hoped that she could avoid the truth coming out.

"No, but here is the thing – who gave Giovanni the letter to give to you? Where is he? And where is my father?" Lorenzo was lost in his thoughts, trying to piece together the limited information that he had.

"What are you thinking, Lorenzo?"

"Something's not adding up here," he replied as he sat down, turning on the small light on the table beside him. The room was suddenly bathed in a warm yellow glow that drowned out the streetlights.

Yvonne watched as Lorenzo made two separate calls on his mobile phone. The first call to Giovanni's mobile indicated the line was dead, and the second one to his father went straight to his voicemail.

Chapter Seventeen

As Yvonne and Lorenzo lay in bed, they were awakened by a polite but persistent knocking at the front door.

"What time is it?" Lorenzo asked sleepily, shielding his eyes from the daylight.

Yvonne looked at the bedside clock. "Almost half-past seven," rubbing her eyes to try and wake up. "God only knows who could want anything now," she muttered drowsily.

"I'll get it," Lorenzo offered, pulling on his trousers. As he stumbled out of the bedroom and opened the front door, Yvonne could hear muffled voices coming from the hallway.

Reappearing in the doorway to the bedroom, Lorenzo's voice wavered, "Yvonne, there are two police officers here to speak to you."

Yvonne's heart began to race, and she gripped the sheets to keep her hands from trembling. "Wh… what, where are they?"

"In the living room."

"What do they want?"

"To speak to you, but they won't say what about." He stood stoically in the doorframe, but his brow was furrowed with worry.

Blood was rushing through Yvonne's ears, deafening any other words Lorenzo may have said and she was sure he would hear her heart trying to burst from her chest. "Right… offer them tea or something. I'll be through in a minute," she replied nervously. "I just need to get covered."

Standing just outside of the living room in her dressing gown, Yvonne tried to compose herself and steady her breathing before walking into the room. She took a deep breath and strode confidently in.

"Good morning," she smiled.

"Yvonne Duncan?" queried one of the policemen, as he turned around from looking out of the window. "I am Detective

Constable Russell, and this is my colleague Detective Constable Wallace."

"Yes, I am Yvonne Duncan. Please, take a seat," she gestured around the living room. She watched as the officers sat together on the couch, while she perched opposite them on an armchair.

"Miss Duncan, a number weeks ago, a young lad who had been with his friends in Grove Park died after he went into the River Kelvin on his bike and drowned."

Yvonne feigned sorrow, shaking her head at the tragic loss of a young life. "Yes, I heard the reports about the boy. So sad… but what has that to do with me?" She was careful to avoid sounding remorseful lest it appeared as guilt.

"Well, we collected statements from all of his friends and he was flirting with an older female."

"Constable, you'll forgive me asking again, but what has that got to do with me?" *Don't let them see you sweat*, she thought to herself.

"We have spent weeks attempting to identify people who were in the area, primarily around the gallery, at the time. Despite an appeal for witnesses, nobody has come forward. However, from CCTV footage we have now traced almost everyone who was there."

DC Russell opened an envelope and pulled out a printed image which he handed to Yvonne.

"Is that you Miss Duncan?"

"Yes," she confirmed without hesitation.

"So you can confirm you were in the park about the time and on the date printed on the photograph? Can you tell us about anything suspicious you may have seen?"

"I often walk through the grounds of the art gallery to relax, especially after a long day at work. That looks like where this was taken," she answered with conviction. *Keep it simple, she reminded herself.*

"Did you see kids on their bikes that evening?"

"There are always kids on their bikes around that bit, practising in the BMX area. I wouldn't be able to tell one from the other."

"Have you ever stopped and spoken to them?"

"Not that I can think of. Definitely not recently, but that track has been there for years so maybe in the past," she replied calmly. Despite her calm exterior, her insides were screaming as panic continued to build.

"Have you ever been followed by any of the boys?" asked DC Wallace, interjecting for the first time since they started questioning her. He was a small spindly man, with a pinched face and deep-set eyes that unnerved her.

"Not that I know of."

"Shouted at? We all know how young lads can be around an attractive woman," he probed, trying to find a misstep in her explanation that would unravel her.

"Don't you think I'm a little out of their age range?"

Aware of the rhetoric nature of her question, both officers side-stepped it without comment.

Instead, DC Russell pulled out a notepad and said, "Once we get your full details, we shall leave you to get on with your day."

He tapped the pad with a pen, indicating that she should provide the details that he had just asked for.

She wrote out both her mobile and office phone numbers underneath her name, the very picture of innocence.

"Thank you very much. We shall be in touch if we need to speak to you again."

They all stood up simultaneously and Yvonne walked with them to the front door. "I'm sorry that I can't be of more assistance to you gentlemen," she stated.

She was hoping to instil them with the sense that she had nothing left to say about the disappearance of 'Mike the Bike', that she was just a stressed-out businesswoman who went for evening walks in the park.

"Oh, you did just fine thank you," commented DC Russell as the two officers left the house.

As he heard the front door click shut, Lorenzo joined Yvonne in the living room slumped in the chair she had just been interrogated in.

"What was all that about Yvonne?"

Lorenzo moved quietly through the room and crouched in front of her. Worry danced through his eyes, and he stared at her imploringly, willing her to let him in. He held onto her legs gently, reassuring her that he was there if she needed him.

"Well, you were here, so you know as much as me." She crossed her arms and stared resolutely out of the window as if he were not directly in front of her.

"Yeah, right." Suspicion coloured his tone, raised by her dismissive attitude.

She turned her attention back to him, her gaze softening. "I'm going to phone the office and tell Anne that I'll be in later. Let's go somewhere for breakfast. I have something to tell you."

They sat on opposite sides of a small wooden table in one of Yvonne's favourite cafés where she used to have breakfast when she had first started her business. It was a tiny place with an unassuming front and only three tables, easily missed if you did not know where to look for it. Yvonne and Lorenzo both had a big mug of tea, and a plate of scrambled eggs, bacon, and toast in front of them. The cutlery was untouched, and the eggs were beginning to cool and congeal as they both waited for the other to initiate the conversation.

"What do you need to tell me that brings us here at this time of the morning?" Lorenzo asked wearily, the look in his eyes matching the tone of his voice.

Yvonne stared unseeingly at the back of Lorenzo's hand lying flat on the table and started to stroke it with her finger before shaking herself from her reverie.

"I don't want you to say anything while I explain, please," she said quietly as she looked around, noting that they were the only two customers. "Don't be angry with me either. No matter what happens, I love you. I want you to know that."

She paused as she took a sip of her tea. Lorenzo noticed that she held little eye contact and had the faintest tremor in her hand, so different from the normally calm and collected woman Lorenzo was used to. Seeing Yvonne rattled disturbed him. She looked out of the café window at the bus stances, watching the steady stream of morning commuters getting off and on of buses, while others headed for the nearby train and subway stations. The city was waking up.

"Are you going to end our relationship, Yvonne?" Lorenzo interjected.

"Oh, no. No. Please, that's not what this is about." She took his hand in her own. "Although there is a possibility that you may end it in a few moments."

"I don't understand, Yvonne." He sat stony-faced, unwilling to fall apart in public.

"I sold Yvonne Duncan Publications," she announced.

That was not what he had expected to hear.

"Can I ask who you sold your company to?" Acting as if he did not already know, his heart ached at her betrayal, at her lack of integrity.

"To your father."

She watched as Lorenzo inhaled deeply, puffing out his cheeks, before exhaling slowly and noisily as he shook his head from side to side.

"Please say something," she pleaded, gripping his hand so hard that her knuckles gleamed white.

"What can I say? It is – or I should say was – your company. You built it, you made it the success it was, and you got to decide what happened to it. Although you know what I thought when I listened to you on the phone to him the other day? 'Here is

168

someone who will finally stand up to my father and not let him get his way.' That's something that I can't even do."

He paused, looking over Yvonne's shoulder for a second before his eyes met hers again. For the first time in their relationship, the conversation was strained, and it was taking a toll on both of them.

"Can I wind the clock back a bit, please?" asked Lorenzo.

"Yes," she responded, taking a small bite of her toast. She was not hungry, and her stomach turned at the food, but she needed to do something with her hands to relieve the anxiety that she was feeling.

"The carry-on with Giovanni and you. You know what I am talking about?"

She blushed so fiercely that her face turned the same colour as her hair.

"I know that it's in the past, it's gone, and I want you to know that I trust you. But what I can't get my head around is that he ended up in a flat opposite you. Secondly, he follows you around. Thirdly, he ends up at my father's house in Sardinia while we are there, and he is the one sent to deliver the envelope to you with the offer for your company. This whole thing stinks, there are too many 'convenient coincidences'."

"Okay, go on," prompted Yvonne, watching Lorenzo's eyes narrow as was his habit when he was thinking.

Lorenzo wondered, *did Giovanni have use of the jet, hence the reason it's at Glasgow Airport?*

"Yvonne, I need to make a call. I'll be a minute, so eat your breakfast before the egg gets stone cold."

Yvonne watched as Lorenzo made a quick exit from the café, taking a bite of his toast as he left. He paced back and forth on the pavement as he spoke on his phone, his wild hand gestures signalling his frustration. He hung up and turned back towards the café and sank into the booth, deflated.

"Lorenzo, are you alright?"

"No, not really."

"Why?"

After swallowing a large gulp of tea, he replied, "I spoke to Maria. Nobody has seen my father in a few days. As for Gio, he got a scheduled flight back to the UK after we left Sardinia, presumably with the letter. So, he had no use of the jet, but it's here, and only one person is allowed to use it. So, my father must be here in Glasgow."

Yvonne's heart ached to see Lorenzo so distressed. She knew it was dangerous, but she had to let him in. "I can see that you are suffering so I'm going… to break a confidentiality clause."

"What does that mean?" asked Lorenzo, looking up at her in surprise.

"If your father gets wind of this I am finished, do you understand? I know blood is thicker than water Lorenzo but please, say nothing. I can't emphasise this enough."

She hoped that her pleading would endear him to her. She took a deep breath. "Your father was here the day before yesterday."

Lorenzo's mouth hung open in shock. He sat up slowly and his eyes narrowed accusingly as the information sank in.

"How do you know that?"

Yvonne met his gaze steadily. "I met him. He was in your flat."

She sat waiting for his reaction.

"Wh… wait a minute, I have to get things straight here," he stammered and his voice raised slightly as he processed this revelation. "You saw my father here? In my flat? Two days ago?" He covered his face with his hands.

"Yes."

"Did you arrange to meet him there?"

"No."

"So who let him into my flat?" he asked accusingly.

Yvonne pulled away from him, she had not expected this barrage of questions and she had not learned how to contend with this side of Lorenzo just yet.

"I don't know who let him in. It was the day that you came into the office to speak with Gordon. I headed over to yours after work as we agreed, and when I got there, he was just sitting in the living room waiting. I don't know how he knew where I was going to be, but it was me that he wanted to speak to."

"I'm listening,"

"He was not pleased in the slightest that I had rejected his offer for my company."

Lorenzo's body language softened at that. "I understand what you're saying. I have seen that spiel of his many times before."

"Well, he made an increased offer with additional conditions."

"The conditions being?"

Here Yvonne decided to draw a line. She was unwilling to get Lorenzo into any more trouble than he was already in, so he reached over and took his hand, signalling that it was not a trust issue, but rather the fact that she loved him and was trying to protect him.

"That, Lorenzo, is between me and your father, subject to severe penalties if disclosed. I've already told you too much, but I wanted you to know. I really couldn't refuse the offer he made."

"You, Miss Duncan, better not be lying to me. I won't ask you about those details, but moving on, you two complete the deal, then what? My father is currently missing, so where did he go after that?"

"He asked me to take him to Glasgow Airport. I assumed he was going home, but thinking about it now, the strange thing is as we came off the M8, onto the slip to the St James' interchange, he asked me to drop him short of the airport itself. He directed me around the roads until we finished up near the airport police office. I left him standing near to some car hire company. I can't remember which one, there are so many over there." Yvonne hesitated then continued, "anyway, that's where I left him. He didn't say why he wanted to change his destination or what he would be doing there, but when he got out of my car he said, and I promise I'll never forget because of the way he said it. 'Enjoy my money, Yvonne, it's the last you shall ever get.' Yvonne spoke slowly as she stared out of the window, reliving those moments in her head.

For the first time since they met Lorenzo had serious doubts about Yvonne's account of events. He was suddenly exhausted, his energy reserves drained by the eventful morning, and he did not want to talk about it anymore.

"Can you take me to the gym when you head into the office, please?"

"No, you can walk," she quipped, a smile crossing her face for the first time that morning.

A short time later, Yvonne was driving her fiancé to his gym. Out of the corner of her eye, she watched him draw his phone from his pocket. As she stopped at the red traffic light, she glanced over at the mobile just in time to see him dial 'Father'.

A ringtone sounded from within the car and they both jumped, startled at the unexpected noise.

"Is that yours?" quizzed Lorenzo.

"No."

"Stop the car now."

Yvonne obeyed and brought the car to a sudden halt. He got out onto the pavement, holding his mobile phone in his hand as he frantically searched the backseat of the car. Reaching under the seat, he recovered his father's mobile phone. He came back around to the front seat, seething.

"Why is this here?" he demanded, holding his father's mobile phone up to Yvonne's face.

Yvonne glared at him. "Right, get a grip! And this answers the question of why he's not answering his phone, he dropped the stupid thing in here. I told you that I'd given him a lift, so what are you accusing me of?"

He took a deep, shuddering breath as he rationalised the discovery. "You're right, you're right. I'm sorry, this is a start. I'll let Maria know that I have his phone. My charger fits his, so I'll power it up at the gym in case he calls it."

He climbed back into the car and securely placed Leonardo's phone alongside his own in his gym bag.

"Right." Yvonne's response was terse as she concentrated on driving Lorenzo to work. Within a few minutes, she had dropped him off outside the gym for his ten o'clock appointment. They kissed, Lorenzo exited the car and stared after her as she drove away.

Yvonne breezed into the office following her usual routine and greeting. "Morning gang, we'll have a meeting in fifteen minutes as per usual, diaries at the ready."

"Yvonne," interrupted Gordon quietly, nodding towards her office.

One man occupied her seat, swinging from side to side, and another sat upon the seat opposite. One had his elbows resting on the arms of her chair, hands clasped before him, while the other had adopted the same pose, but his forefingers circled each other, perpetually restless. Both were looking in her direction. They resembled vultures, eyeing up a carcass and waiting for the right opportunity to rip it to shreds. She shuddered involuntarily.

"Okay, morning meeting cancelled for the moment," said Yvonne looking directly at the two men. "Take an extended tea break. Let's say an hour – except Gordon, you stay, please. Everyone else, out of the office."

"Yvonne, who are they?" asked Gordon as their co-workers shuffled out, hushed whispers developing theories about what was going on.

She had no answer for him as she walked towards the office.

Chapter Eighteen

Yvonne stood in the doorway looking around her.

"You," she said pointing her finger and in a raised voice, "that is my chair, now get the hell out of it."

"Miss Duncan, that sort of language is not in character for you." Leonardo Maldini regarded her with his steely cold eyes.

"Let me put it this way then." Yvonne paused as she raised her eyes to the ceiling and took a deep breath. "Git yer arse tae hell oot ma chair, pal. Now, dae ye understand that?" Her Glaswegian accent was menacing as she stalked forward, leaning on her desk with her fists clenched beneath her, eyes narrowed, and lips pursed.

"Miss Duncan—" Leonardo began before he was interrupted.

"Don't 'Miss Duncan' me. Up and out of MY chair – then we talk, Mr Maldini."

Leonardo made no attempt to move but calmly regarded her. "Miss Duncan, I bought your company for a sizeable amount of money."

Yvonne remained defensive and imposing over him.

"And today, it has no clients, nothing." He stated, raising his hands and shrugging his shoulders. "Your explanation is what, exactly?"

Yvonne regarded him indifferently from her vantage point above him. "You bought my company name, Mr Maldini. Our contract did not stipulate anything more specific, so I called my clients and because of the level of service I provide, they agreed to terminate their contracts and to come over to Yvonne Duncan and Company."

She paused in her explanation and turned to face the man who was seated to her right. "I am sorry we have not been introduced."

As the stranger stood up for a formal introduction, Yvonne's demeanour suddenly changed from anger to calm, which unnerved Leonardo.

"Yvonne, this is Luca, my brother. He is Lorenzo's uncle."

"Pleased to meet you," she said holding out her hand to Luca, who resembled a six-foot, six-inch, twenty-stone heavyweight boxer of yesteryear, with slicked-back hair and a flat crooked nose.

"I doubt it," he replied curtly. His hands were folded in front of him, and he was glaring down at her hand, refusing to shake it.

"Oh, it's going to be like that, is it?"

"That depends on you," growled Luca, as he sat back down.

Yvonne looked him up and down for a moment, evaluating his stature. "Tell me something Luca – can you swim?"

He stared at her, failing to comprehend the relevance of her question. She sighed in exasperation. "Okay, that was a difficult question for a man of your intelligence, so let's try this one instead. Are you Giovanni's father?

"Si."

"Well, he must take his brains from his mother because he certainly doesn't get them from you," she muttered.

Leonardo Maldini burst into laughter. Unlike his brother, the meaning of her comment was not lost on him. As he gathered himself, he said in his thick Italian accent, "Miss Duncan – Yvonne. We are both business people. I am sure that we can resolve this situation sensibly, like adults."

His arms spread open to her in a deceivingly hospitable gesture as if they were family.

"I am sure we can do that when you get up from my desk."

Gordon observed the event unfolding from the main office, watching as Yvonne refused to budge and the men exchanged glances. They were obviously unsure how to handle this behaviour from a woman. Their body language was small, while Yvonne towered over them and commanded the room. To

Gordon, this had become like a standoff from a movie with a classic power struggle, except it was his boss who was standing up to the Mafia. It was surreal.

He picked up the telephone on his desk and dialled a number from his computer screen. "Get yourself over here immediately, I think Yvonne is in trouble," he whispered before replacing the receiver on the cradle.

Back in Yvonne's office, the power struggle continued.

"Well Mr Maldini, I thought that you were a gentleman. While you and 'Guy the Gorilla' lounge about, I have to stand. That is really no way to treat a lady," she tutted.

A smile slowly spread across Leonardo's face, and he dipped his head in acknowledgement. He pushed the chair back from the desk and rose to his feet. Standing to one side, he gestured towards the chair and invited her to sit. Yvonne walked around her desk and sat down. Leonardo glanced at Luca who immediately stood and offered up his seat – the pecking order of the Maldini family was quite clear.

"Mr Maldini, lets you and I have a conversation in private so we can resolve this," suggested Yvonne from her reclaimed office chair.

"Lasciaci soli, starò bene. Aspetto fuori," instructed Leonardo, signalling for his brother to leave the office with a nod of his head.

"What did you just say to him?"

"'Leave us alone, I shall be okay. Wait outside," translated Lorenzo who had materialised in the office doorway.

"Lorenzo, what are you doing here?" gasped Yvonne.

"I got a call. Hello, Father. Uncle Luca, it's been a while." He acknowledged each man in turn before walking up to his father and looked him straight in the eyes. "What is going on, Father? Where have you been? We've all been worried about you."

"Lorenzo, why would you be worried about me? Did you think I was sleeping with the fishes?" Leonardo asked, flashing a look at Yvonne. "I decided to book into a hotel here in this wonderful city and take in the sights, then I found that I had lost my phone like a stupid old man, so I contacted Luca to meet me."

"I have your phone, you dropped it in Yvonne's car."

"Ah good, thank you for returning it to me, Lorenzo. You can be a good son after all," he remarked, carefully choosing words that would sting. The jibe had hit its mark as a look of pain flashed briefly over Lorenzo's face.

"Now, if you shall all excuse me for a few moments while I visit the restroom," announced Leonardo as he left the room.

When Leonardo re-entered the room, he clicked the door shut behind him and took the vacant chair in front of Yvonne and beside Lorenzo. They stared at each other, each unwilling to break the silence first. To speak first would be weak, and neither of them could afford that.

"Right. Enough is enough," sighed Lorenzo. He was not in the same position as his fiancée or his father, so he decided to act as a mediator. "What is going on here?"

Leonardo ignored his son and stared steadfastly at Yvonne. "Miss Duncan, earlier you accused me of not being a gentleman by not giving up a chair to a lady, so now, I am going to be a gentleman and allow you to speak first. I suggest that you tell my son exactly what you have done," he said smugly. His move was calculated and granted him control over the situation.

Yvonne drew her chair close to her desk and raised it ever-so-slightly, just enough that she was looking down over the men in the room. It was a technique that she had perfected over the years, indicating her confidence.

"Lorenzo, we had a discussion over breakfast about your father buying Yvonne Duncan Publications."

"Yes."

"And from what you said to me, you were disappointed in me."

Lorenzo looked embarrassed and shuffled slightly in his chair. "To be honest… yes."

"Well, the bit I did not get to explain to you was that," she paused, looking pointedly at Leonardo, "when I sold the company to your father, we – my staff and I – called all our clients; the authors, the editors, the illustrators, everyone, to tell them that Yvonne Duncan Publications was under new ownership and that I had started a new company. I registered Yvonne Duncan and Company as a limited company years ago. What happened next was that all clients associated with Yvonne Duncan Publications terminated their contracts and have moved their business to my new company. I did not terminate their contracts. They terminated the contracts, which they are well within their rights to do, as stated in their earlier Yvonne Duncan Publications agreements. They were not employees, and everything was done on a book-to-book basis. As I have explained to your father, I informed them of a management change, and they have decided to follow me to my new company of their own volition because they know that I deliver on service."

"So, what does that all mean?" asked Lorenzo.

"It means that all I have is this," snarled Leonardo as he gestured around the office, "to show for one-point-five-million euros of my own money."

Yvonne interjected with a slight correction. "Well Mr Maldini, I regret to inform you, but you don't have this either. This office space is rented under my own name, not under Yvonne Duncan Publications."

"So, what do I own Miss Duncan?" Leonardo's tone was venomous, and he could scarcely contain his anger at this new revelation. He sat opposite Yvonne, hatred sparking in his eyes as he calculated exactly how he had been outdone.

"You own Yvonne Duncan Publications, as per our contract. You own the name, and you have the staff if you wish to keep them, and they wish to stay. The thing is, they have nothing to do, and you will have to pay them or make them redundant.

However, as a gesture of goodwill, I shall take them off your hands with immediate effect."

"Where does this leave you financially, Father?" interjected Lorenzo.

"Not great on this side of the business, but I shall manage," he muttered, recognising his defeat.

"Okay," announced Yvonne suddenly, as if she had only just thought of her forthcoming suggestion. "I am prepared to offer you one-million euros for a seventy-five per cent share in your fitness centres."

"Yvonne, are you mad?" whispered Lorenzo out of the side of his mouth.

"No. I know to the penny what that chain of business is worth. I had it checked out by my lawyers and, unlike your father's lawyers, mine are thorough."

She reached down to a lower drawer in her desk and withdrew an A4 brown envelope, which she threw in front of Leonardo. "Mr Maldini, I am sure that you have direct contact with your lawyers wherever they are in Italy. I am also sure that Lorenzo will let you borrow his phone to call them. I will send my staff home for the day, giving you free rein of all the equipment you may need here. Now, let me see... since all this started, a significant portion of time has already gone by. I shall return the favour you gave me, but I will be a little more lenient than you were because I love your son. She paused, looking at her watch, "It's now eleven twenty-one a.m., so using London Time, from three p.m., every minute that the contract is not signed on my desk shall cost you fifty-thousand euros."

"And if I refuse?" he countered.

"Well, you own Yvonne Duncan Publications, so it's entirely up to you, Mr Maldini, and the clock is ticking. I'll get Gordon to log you on to that computer over there just in case you need to use it."

Leonardo shuffled out of Yvonne's office and into the main space, his head down and his fists dug deeply into his pockets.

"Gordon," Yvonne instructed, "If Mr Maldini needs assistance on the computer, please help him as best you can."

"Certainly," came the disembodied reply before she closed the door, isolating herself and Lorenzo in the smaller glass office.

"I'm cancelling my classes for today," declared Lorenzo.

"Why?" she asked, somewhat bewildered.

"There is no way that I am leaving you here with the two of them. Although… you are worse than the two of them put together," he teased looking out of the office towards his father and uncle.

He turned his attention back to Yvonne and held her hand. "You held your own and I'm very attracted to you when you own your power."

"Do you fancy lunch at one o'clock?" purred Yvonne and she glanced at him flirtatiously, lapping up his affection.

"What, do you fancy?" he replied.

"With that tone of voice, are you available?" she asked mischievously.

"Definitely," he said smiling. "Your place or mine?"

As they left the office, Yvonne looked over at Leonardo and Luca who were on the phones, frantically discussing something in Italian. Lorenzo looked at both men and smiled, picking up on the conversations they were having.

When they got outside, Yvonne asked what was being said.

"Well, from what I could hear, they were in contact with their respective lawyers. It seems like yours have already been in touch."

"Lovely," she said as she kissed his cheek.

"What time is it?" asked Yvonne a while later.

"Almost two o'clock."

"Wouldn't it be nice just to stay here for the rest of the day?" she sighed as she rolled over, pulling the duvet up and wrapping her arm around Lorenzo's body.

"Yeah, but don't you have a company to take control of this afternoon?" He grinned at her, kissing the top of her head with pride.

"Mmmm, I would rather have control of you," she whispered as she reached up to meet his lips.

"Gentlemen. How are things progressing?" asked Yvonne as she sauntered back into the main office.

"Where is Lorenzo?" demanded Leonardo.

"He had a few things to clear up at the flat."

Yvonne glanced at Gordon whose head was bowed as he pretended to be busy at his desk, but his eyes were raised, and he watched her go into her office. A slight smile spread over his face as he began to clear out paperwork with the old company logo and headings.

Leonardo followed her into her office and stood at her desk.

"We need some more time, Yvonne," he pleaded.

"Mr Maldini, you still have just over thirty minutes," she stated as she checked her watch.

"Would you invoke the penalty clauses if we missed the deadline?"

"Of course. You would have done it to me."

"I wonder what Luca and Lorenzo would say if they knew the truth about Giovanni. How would you get out of that one?" he said his tone quiet and threatening.

"By telling them that you are a vindictive old man, only angry because a woman pulled one over on you and that you haven't a hope in hell of proving what you're saying. It's simply not true."

"But we both know that I am not lying, correct?" replied Leonardo.

"Be careful, Mr Maldini, and I mean, be very careful. You may be the father of my fiancé, but that would not get in the way of you 'sleeping with the fishes'. I take it you understand?"

He blinked, turned around, and walked out of the room, when he reached the doorway he glanced back, his face was purple with rage.

Chapter Nineteen

Later that day as Yvonne sat working at her desk, she glanced up to see Leonardo Maldini again.

"Miss Duncan, check your emails."

"What am I looking for?"

She did not need to ask, 'CONTRACT' jumped out at her as soon as her inbox opened up.

Leonardo watched as her eyes scanned the contents of the email, taking in the terms of the sale laid out in the contract. An electronic signature was all that was needed to complete the transaction.

Yvonne leaned back in her chair, her hands clasped in front of her. She waited several moments before speaking until Leonardo was visibly uncomfortable, and she had the upper hand.

"Tell me something, Leonardo," she demanded, staring at the screen. "If I had sent this to you, would you sign it?"

"Yes."

"Why?"

"Because I would be getting seventy-five per cent of a company for a very cheap price."

Yvonne nodded, digesting his response. She picked up her office telephone, and never breaking eye contact with Leonardo, called her lawyer. A flurry of conversation explaining what had been laid out in the contract followed.

Finally, she asked, "Is this all good?"

She listened nodding her head and she continued to stare at Leonardo, nodding occasionally. She hung up and motioned for Leonardo to sit.

Leonardo had not moved at all throughout her phone call, but now he quietly did as he was told

"Now Yvonne, what are your plans for my company?"

"I think you mean our company, for that's what it will be if I press this button."

"Yes, okay, our company."

Yvonne smiled at the correction. "I'm going to give my share to Lorenzo as a wedding present. I'm assuming you will give him the rest when the time comes, and he will be the sole owner. We'll live exceedingly well off of the profits."

"Do you honestly think I would allow that to happen?" Leonardo asked menacingly. He refused to believe that their engagement was anything more than a farce, but more important than that he refused to accept that he lacked the upper hand in their current situation.

"You have no say in this matter. Also, please be aware that in the next few minutes, contractual penalties begin to come into effect. You may not want to test me just now." Her eyes blazed at the audacity he displayed by interfering in her relationship.

"But you have opened the email, everyone knows you are looking at it, so if you want the contract and the deal, sign it. I have done nothing outside of what you have asked."

"This is true, but I can always wait before I sign it if you're not thrilled at the idea of having me as a daughter-in-law."

She stared and Leonardo's shoulders slumped. He gave a single, sad nod, admitting his defeat.

"Well Mr Maldini, it has been a pleasure doing business with you." With a single click of her mouse, their deal was sealed.

"Would you like to check your account, Mr Maldini?"

"No, I trust you," he sighed. "Do you know something, if you had been a man in my homeland, you would have been a Capo at the very least, if not the Capo tutti I Capi... or possibly dead."

"What does that mean?" *And I really need to learn Italian if I'm going to be part of this family,* she thought dryly to herself.

"It means that you have my respect, Miss Duncan," he explained cryptically in a low voice.

"I don't quite know how to take that," she replied. She had never expected to be complimented, let alone respected by this Mafia man.

"Take it as a badge of honour, Miss Duncan. Take it as a badge of honour from a Capo. If you do not understand, ask Lorenzo," he said as he held out his hand. It was a gesture performed in one way as a business partner and on some level, in friendship.

As they shook hands, Yvonne asked. "Do you know why I have done this? I did it to prove to you that women are no pushovers, so when you go home, respect your wife and your daughter. They are just as strong as you and me. And your son, you treat him like a servant, but he runs your companies over here and makes you rich. You should have the same respect for him as you do for me. Now go home, Leonardo, and take that gorilla out there with you." She commanded, releasing his hand.

Leonardo bowed his head slightly, like someone offering respect at a funeral, before leaving the office with his brother.

Yvonne called out to Gordon from her office, "Do you fancy a drink? I've got a nice decanter of whisky back here."

He approached her door. "I'm working."

"You are officially finished as of now."

"Well, in that case, I got the train into work today, so why not?" He grinned at her as he took the seat that Leonardo had just vacated.

Yvonne poured two large whiskies from a decanter that was tucked away behind her desk.

They sat in silence for a few minutes, and Yvonne could see that Gordon was troubled by the way that he constantly swirled his whisky around his glass. "

Okay, what's bothering you?"

Gordon sighed and took a big sip of the smooth, single malt whisky.

"As I said days, or maybe weeks ago, I don't remember and it doesn't matter now, I did a little research on the Maldini family."

185

"Yes, you said."

"Yvonne… do you have any idea who you have just screwed over?" he asked, clutching his whisky glass.

She simply shrugged her shoulders.

Gordon peered surreptitiously around him, worried that they may be overheard in the empty office. "You have just screwed over a leading member of the Mafia."

He downed the rest of his whisky as Yvonne contemplated what Leonardo had said earlier and how it fit with what Gordon was telling her now. The extensive wealth, the many businesses, whatever his job as a Capo was…

"I'm heading home if that's okay?" Gordon asked interrupting her thought process.

"Sure, I have a few things to do, preparing for Yvonne Duncan and Company. I'll lock up."

"When does this company come into effect, boss?"

"No time like the present, Gordon. First thing in the morning." She smiled at him, showing how grateful she was for his constant support.

As Gordon walked downstairs a dark-eyed, swarthy man in his mid-thirties began to pass him on the stairs then stopped abruptly.

"Excuse me."

Gordon stopped in his tracks.

"I have an appointment with… let me check," he paused, drawing a piece of paper from his pocket. "Yvonne Duncan? Do you know where her offices are, please?" There was a slight Italian accent to his voice.

Gordon's bullshit radar kicked into the full force, and he lied effortlessly to the phoney standing next to him. "No, sorry mate. She left here a few hours ago, the company has been sold so the offices are closed."

The man changed his original direction and accompanied Gordon down the stairs. "Did you work for her?"

"Yeah, for years, then she just got up and walked out, left us with nothing. No job, nothing."

"That's a shame for you. But thank you for letting me know," the man acknowledged with a nod of his head.

Safely outside and on his own, Gordon leaned against the brick wall, the adrenaline of the encounter quickly fading. He closed his eyes, knowing that something was wrong and that Yvonne was in danger. It was simply a gut feeling he had. He looked around as he took the phone from his pocket, but he couldn't see the man he had spoken to on the stairs anywhere.

"Gordon?" asked Yvonne down the phone.

"Yvonne, either something is wrong, or I'm paranoid after today's events."

"What is it, Gordon?"

Listening intently to his story as he recounted what had just happened, including a description of who he had just spoken to. Yvonne flipped through her memory bank of men who might match that description, but she had to admit that she did not recognise him.

"Thank you. Go home and enjoy your evening, Gordon, I'll see you tomorrow."

Long after the phone call was done, Yvonne's mind was still ticking over as to who the man could be – or who he had been sent by. She could only come to one conclusion: that he was linked to the Maldini family. He did not sound that different to the Mediterranean men she had seen in Sardinia. She did not want to admit it, but she was afraid to leave the office. As she got ready to head home, she checked her bag methodically. Laptop, phone, purse, make-up bag, locking knife, car keys, house keys, all present and accounted for. Her senses were heightened after the call from Gordon, and as she got into her Audi, she locked the car doors before driving home.

Driving down Argyle Street towards Dumbarton Road, her eyes constantly strayed to her rear-view mirror. One car had been with her since she left the office, and she was becoming increasingly wary. *Okay, let's see how this goes,* she thought as she turned the vehicle into Clayslaps Road. Clayslaps Road was a short road that connected Argyle Street to Sauchiehall Street. Not many cars usually traveled down but as she drove on, the car behind did the same. She stopped at the junction before turning onto Sauchiehall Street. Kelvin Way was on her left, but she intentionally did not indicate which way she was going.

Red turned to amber, amber turned to green, and as Yvonne released the clutch, she quickly turned onto Kelvin Way. The other car did not hesitate in following. Again, without indicating, she turned into the access road to The Grove Art Gallery, coming to a halt in a marked parking bay. The vehicle that followed her did likewise, continually mimicking her movements. Yvonne's skin prickled in fear mixed with anticipation. Before getting out of her car, she reached into her bag and removed the locking knife, putting it into her right-hand pocket for easy access.

Only the small streetlights around the museum lit the area as Yvonne stepped from her car, bathing it in a muted orange glow which was just enough light to see by. She was aware of the security cameras around her as she made her way towards Grove Park across Kelvin Way. The popular biking area to her left was empty and young Michael Bradley, the kid who had drowned in the River Kelvin, suddenly surfaced in her memories.

As she made her way to the pavilion, she knew she was being followed, and she was certain that it was the driver of the mysterious car, but was he the same man who Gordon had seen on the stairs? What did he want with her? There were too many questions and not enough answers.

Stopping at the pavilion, she leaned against the wall and saw a figure coming closer, approaching her from the murky blackness of the poorly illuminated park. Her right hand was firmly wrapped around her locking knife, kept safely out of sight in her deep coat pocket.

"Yvonne Duncan?" A disembodied voice floated through the air, a voice matching the one that threatened her in the car park all those nights ago.

"Who wants to know?" she replied coolly. Her heartbeat had quickened in fear, but her poise remained strong, unwavering.

"I am a friend of Leonardo Maldini. He has asked a little favour of me. I have been sent here to end your life so that you cannot marry his son and he can reclaim his business. I think you have the right to know that before you die." The voice was calm and matter-of-fact.

Although she was not surprised, her heart still skipped a beat in primal fear. "Thank you," she responded calmly. "I appreciate your honesty."

He slid his hand inside his jacket.

"Hey, what's the rush," she purred in a low voice, pushing herself off the wall and walking towards him slowly. Before she left the car, she had put on a pair of knee-high leather boots on. Her eyes narrowed as she surveyed him admiring her legs.

"Do I get a last request?" she asked, gazing longingly into the killer's eyes. She batted her eyelashes seductively.

"Depends what it is." His voice was a gruff growl.

"I want to have sex one last time. Come here and kiss me," she invited huskily.

Yvonne slowly undid the buttons on her sheer red blouse revealing the plunging line of her silk bra and the swell of her cleavage.

The assassin approached her warily, but his eyes were fixated on the heaving of her chest. Taking advantage of his distraction, she grabbed the locking knife from her pocket and slashed through his throat, with as little resistance as softened butter. The cut was deep enough to ensure death within minutes. Her assailant dropped to his knees while clutching his neck, his hands coated in a glistening crimson, beautifully catching the minimal light of the dark evening.

Stepping over the still, lifeless body Yvonne hurried over to the River Kelvin, where the bloody locking knife sank into its murky depths.

A short time later Yvonne stepped out of the shower and she made a phone call.

"Lorenzo, do you want to spend the night here? I'm in the mood for my fiancé."

"Oh, have you been bad again?" he replied. From down the phone, Yvonne could hear his breathing quicken.

"Yes, I have," she answered her voice low and filled with sexual longing.

"Tell me something," Yvonne asked as she lay naked on top of Lorenzo, lazily tracing her finger across his smooth, chiselled chest. "What is a Capo?" she asked quietly.

"A Capo, in Italian, is a boss."

"And a Capo tutti I Capi?"

He raised his eyebrows at the question, before answering. "A Capo tutti I Capi is… how do I put this," began Lorenzo. "The Mafia is split into what is known as families. Each family has a boss, a Capo. Hold on, I'm trying to think of a way of keeping this simple. Let's say Glasgow has six gangs, and each gang has their own boss. Then there is the big boss, he is number one, he is the boss of all bosses, the Capo tutti I Capi. Does that make sense?"

His arms wrapped tightly around Yvonne as she rested her head on his chest.

"Yes, I was just reading up on some things, and I needed you to tell me to be sure." She paused. "Lorenzo?"

"What?"

"Is your dad connected to the Mafia?"

"Absolutely not! Why the hell would you ask a question like that?" he exclaimed indignantly.

"Let me explain," Yvonne soothed. "Today after everything that happened, I made a call to my lawyer. Now, depending on your answer to my question, what I have requested will become legal."

"Yvonne you are speaking in riddles, again." He sat up and crossed his arms over his chest.

"I love you, and I want to marry you. I know that we're engaged, but I want it to be more than that. I don't want to wait."

"Yvonne Duncan, are you asking me for a quickie wedding?" He rolled her over onto her back.

"Yes, I am." Yvonne snuggled seductively beneath his welcome form.

"Now, let me see," he replied, "does this mean I have to get rid of my fan club?"

"With immediate effect," she grinned.

"Yes, I would love to be your husband."

"How do you fancy a secret wedding? None of all that big stuff."

"Are you serious?"

"Of course I am. I know I love you, I know that you love me, so four weeks ago I registered us to get married. We have fulfilled the twenty-nine days notice as required, so we can do it tomorrow if you want." She gazed into his eyes.

"You are something else, Miss Duncan. How about midday today, rather than waiting until tomorrow? 'Yvonne Maldini' has a nice ring to it, don't you think?" He moved his lips and tongue over her lips and down her neck.

"I love it as much as I love you."

Yvonne dialled the number for Glasgow City Chambers with Lorenzo next to her.

"Good morning. Is it possible to get married today? We have fulfilled all the legal requirements of notification to marry."

"Please let me check our diary." There was a pause and Yvonne heard the click of fingers on a keyboard.

"We have a cancellation at three o'clock today, will that work for you?"

"Yes, that's perfect. Yvonne Duncan to Lorenzo Maldini at three o'clock."

"Wonderful. That's you booked in. Be here thirty minutes before the ceremony, and congratulations to you both."

"Thank you so much!"

She turned her attention to her soon-to-be-husband. His hair was messy, and his eyes sparkled with excitement. He was so handsome, and she fell in love with him all over again.

"Now, Mr Maldini. The question, is, do we lie here until it's time to get married or do we go to work?"

"To hell with work," he murmured as he moved down her body.

After a well-spent morning, the satiated couple were ravenous and wandered to the kitchen.

"TV or radio?" he asked, while she got out the pots and pans for their breakfast.

"Radio will do, get the news in a couple of minutes."

"Cassandra, play Radio Scotland please," he requested. The high-tech virtual assistant came to life from the corner music playing softly.

"Do you know what I'm going to make?" Yvonne asked. "I'm going to make us a wedding morning breakfast."

"What the hell is that?" he laughed as he wrapped his arms around her from behind and kissed her neck.

"Toasted bread, asparagus, and poached eggs on top of fresh salmon, all covered with hollandaise sauce." She detailed as she leaned into him.

"Okay... if you say so."

"Trust me, this is delicious."

Later, Lorenzo pushed his chair back from the table and admitted that breakfast had been tasty. "How often do I get this," he asked.

"What? Me or the salmon?"

"Both," he replied with a smile.

"Uh oh, we need witnesses for today," muttered Yvonne as she realised they had to find two people for three o'clock that afternoon, her brain immediately kicking into problem-solving mode. "Gordon for sure, but what about you?"

"I'm going to get someone off the street."

Yvonne shot him an exasperated look as she dialled Gordon's number.

"Gordon, I need a favour. Can you meet Lorenzo and me at the Glasgow registry office at half-past two this afternoon?"

She nodded as he spoke. "That's great, thank you."

Yvonne disconnected and placed her phone on the table. "So, that's Gordon sorted for this afternoon. Are you seriously just going to pick someone off the street?"

Their discussions were interrupted by Cassandra. "This is the BBC Radio Scotland news at eleven o'clock. Police Scotland are appealing for witnesses to come forward, following the discovery of a body at the Pavillion in Grove Park in the early hours of this morning. It is believed to be a man in his late twenties to early thirties. Police have declined to say how the man died and inquiries are ongoing. Now onto the other news…" The announcer's voice trailed off into nothingness as Yvonne manually turned down the sound.

"This city is getting worse for murders." She commented staring out of the kitchen window, then shook herself back to the present. After a moment she turned to Lorenzo. "Now Lorenzo, off to your place, you can't be with the bride this early. It's bad luck to see me before the wedding."

"Okay, see you there." Lorenzo gave her a swift kiss as he got up to get dressed.

At half-past two, Yvonne, Lorenzo and Gordon stood outside the registry office in Glasgow city centre. Lorenzo kept looking around at anyone and everyone who walked past them.

"Lorenzo, what are you doing?"

"Looking for someone else to be a witness," he explained.

He spotted an elderly lady, with neat, short white hair framing a lightly lined face and bright blue eyes. She carried her shopping bags easily as she walked towards them.

Lorenzo approached her with his mesmerising smile. "Excuse me, ma'am, when was the last time you were at a wedding?"

"Oh son, the last wedding I was at that was years ago. It's mainly funerals now. They're not such lively events," she tutted as she stopped for a chat.

"Right. See this beautiful woman? I am marrying her at three o'clock. I would be most happy if you would attend."

"Aye, that would be lovely." She gazed up at Lorenzo in delight and tried to clap her hands, but they were tangled in the shopping bags.

"What's your name?"

"Sadie, son. Sadie Reilly."

"Okay, Sadie Reilly, bring your shopping. You are going to a wedding." He beamed at her, proving to Yvonne that his plan had worked.

"Whit's your name, hen?" asked Sadie as she turned to inspect the bride-to-be.

"Yvonne."

"Whit about you pal?"

"I'm Gordon. Do you need help with those bags?" he asked, ever the gentleman as they all prepared to enter the building.

"Dinnae worry pal, I'll manage. So, see this wedding. Are youse aw getting married? You know whit it's like nooadays."

"No," explained Lorenzo laughing, "you and Gordon are going as witnesses. It's just Yvonne and I getting married."

"Oh, so I'm like a bridesmaid?"

"Yeah, just like a bridesmaid Sadie."

Yvonne smiled as they all got to know each other. Sadie was charming and Yvonne thought that Lorenzo may have been right to choose his witness spontaneously.

"Whit's yer name again son?"

"Lorenzo."

"Lorenzo? Is that foreign or something?"

"It's Italian, Sadie."

She paused. "Italian? Like fae Italy?"

"Aye, like fae Italy," replied Lorenzo in his best Glaswegian accent.

"That's great son your English is awfy good" she replied, sending Lorenzo into hysterics.

"Lorenzo, how long is this going to take?" asked Sadie, who had decided that Lorenzo was the most interesting of the three.

"A few minutes more Sadie, then we're in next."

"Miss Duncan, Mr Maldini," called the registrar's assistant right on cue. "This way, please."

The four were ushered into a small, sparsely decorated room that was bathed in harsh UV lighting.

"Excuse me, hen," said Sadie to the assistant, "how long is this going to take?"

"Not long," came the assistant's blunt reply.

"It's just ah huv frozen stuff in ma bags, like fish fingers. Ye know whit ah mean hen its ma mans' tea?"

By half-past three, Mr and Mrs Maldini emerged from the registrar's office with their witnesses.

"Sadie, you have been a star. I hope you enjoyed yourself," beamed Lorenzo.

"Och aye son, that was lovely. Wait until I tell ma man whit happened."

Lorenzo reached into his pocket and handed Sadie some money.

"Listen, son, ah don't want that," she exclaimed, handing it back to him. "Go get yersels' a drink on me. See me, I'm fae Glesga, and no like you foreigners, we help everybody. Good luck, hen," she shouted to Yvonne as she tottered down the road, her shopping bags rustling.

Lorenzo and Yvonne hung onto each other with newlywed bliss.

"Guys, I have a job to get to so I'll leave you to it," announced Gordon, "but I'll see you in the office tomorrow, Yvonne?"

"Yes. Thank you, Gordon."

"Yeah, and that goes for me as well," said Lorenzo, shaking hands with Gordon before he walked away. He turned his attention back to his new bride.

"Right, Mrs Maldini, it's home time."

"Now there is a thing. Where is home?"

"Wherever you want it to be," he replied.

"For today, it's your place, Mr Maldini." She smiled as they wandered down towards Merchant's City, disrupting the flow of foot traffic, unable to let go of each other.

As daylight faded, the couple were completely unaware that someone had been watching their every move, relaying the details back to Sardinia across the phone.

"No more mistakes," was the tinny reply. The call ended.

Chapter Twenty

"Good morning, everyone," greeted Yvonne joyfully. "Today is the start of a new chapter – no pun intended – as we officially open Yvonne Duncan and Company for business!"

She went into her office for a matter of minutes before returning to the main office with a bottle of champagne and fluted glasses for each member of her staff. She filled each glass as they stood around Gordon's desk.

"Same old office, same old staff, same old desks, same old routine, but geez are we so much better off than we were last week. So raise your glasses to Yvonne Duncan and Company and you guys who are really the company"

Yvonne's morning speech was interrupted by two smartly dressed men entering the office. She immediately recognised both of them.

"Detective Constable Russell, Detective Constable Wallace. What can I do for you?"

"Good morning Miss Duncan. Can we talk in your office please?"

"Of course," replied Yvonne as the staff looked on, their eyes following the exchange intently.

After she had closed her office door, Yvonne sat behind her desk, "Please sit gentlemen. What can I do for you?"

"You can gather your things together and accompany us to the station," said DC Wallace.

"And why would I do that?"

"We want to interview you concerning a murder that happened two nights ago. You can come voluntarily, or we can detain you, it's your choice."

"I'll come with you voluntarily. I have nothing to hide."

"Thank you, Miss Duncan."

"It's Mrs Maldini now," she corrected confidently.

The officers exchanged a glance.

As she left the office flanked by the officers she requested, "Gordon, please take care of the office."

That instruction to Gordon, from her, signalled she was handing over command to him.

When she arrived at Partick Police Office, only a stone's throw away from her flat, Yvonne looked around as she was taken through to an interview room with a plain wooden desk and matching chairs. Yvonne glanced to her left, two cassettes were in the recorder as this interview was being recorded in full. DC Wallace pushed the record button.

"Mrs Maldini, before we start this interview, do you wish the services of a solicitor?" asked DC Russell.

"Do I need one?"

"Well, you are going to be asked questions concerning a murder, but it is entirely your choice."

"A murder I know nothing about, so I won't bother with a lawyer."

As the taped interview began, all three individuals in the room identified themselves and Yvonne was then cautioned at common law.

"Miss Duncan—" began DC Russell before Yvonne interjected.

"I think that you have forgotten that I am Mrs Maldini now. Please address me with my proper name."

DC Russell glowered at her but continued professionally. "Apologies. Mrs Maldini, I am going to ask you some questions about a murder that took place in Grove Park two nights ago."

"Okay."

"Mrs Maldini, can you state your occupation please?"

"I run my own publishing house and I have recently acquired a chain of gyms in Glasgow and throughout Scotland."

DC Russell looked surprised at her answer. "Can you please tell me where you were two nights ago at about eight o'clock.?"

"It had been a tough day at work, so I was letting off some steam by walking in the park. I had gotten there earlier in the evening, and I was beginning to make my way back to the car around eight."

"Miss Duncan – sorry, Mrs Maldini – do you remember we spoke recently?"

"Yes."

"And can you confirm that that conversation concerned the death of a young lad who died in the River Kelvin?"

"Yes."

"Now, bearing in mind that we have you on video from that evening, and you have been seen on video again when this man died two nights ago in the same park, death seems to follow you. It's a little coincidental, don't you think?"

"I'm sorry, but I seem to be missing something here. Are you suggesting that because I choose to park at the Art Gallery and go for a walk in the park that I am a murderer? I told you before that's how I like to relax after a long day at the office."

"Please let me finish, Mrs Maldini. You see, what I have not revealed is that we have two witnesses to the events that led to the man's death, two witnesses who can place you at the scene of the crime."

Yvonne stared at the detectives, unsure whether they were bluffing or not.

"Do you know anyone by the names of Leonardo and Luca Maldini?"

Yvonne scowled. I've been set up. "Yes," she sighed. "They're related to my husband, Lorenzo Maldini."

"Have you seen them recently?"

"Mrs Maldini." DC Russell said as he leaned forward onto the desk, "we are in an age of technology. Everything is captured on mobile telephones, whether it's day or night. There are cameras are all over this city and your personalised number plate sticks out like a sore thumb. It isn't difficult to track you down."

"What are you saying?"

"Mrs Maldini, I would like to think of myself to be a fair and honourable police officer, so I am going to be straight with you. We have a video of you murdering someone in Grove Park. Police officers in Italy are going to interview Mr Maldini and his brother for their version of events. Can I suggest that you get a lawyer for the next part of this interview?"

"Why?"

"Because," he explained bluntly, "I am going to arrest you for the murder of Riccardo Castanova."

"I've never heard of him."

"Maybe not, but that is the man who was found dead."

Yvonne sighed in defeat then requested, "May I have a break please, then I shall tell you everything."

"Of course," replied DC Russell, pausing the recorder. "Can I get you something?" he asked.

"Coffee, black, no sugar please."

"Sure thing," he acknowledged as he shuffled off.

Ten minutes later, Yvonne had a steaming cup of charcoal coloured coffee in a polystyrene cup in front of her and inhaled the faint scent of weak, watery police coffee.

DC Russell started the proceedings again. "Mrs Maldini, you indicated earlier you wished to tell DC Wallace and me everything that happened in the park. Are you sure that you do not want a lawyer before we continue?"

"Yes. I have nothing to deny, I'm just going to tell the truth. But before I get to last night, there is more you must know.

"It all started a few months ago. One night, I was down at the mouth of Loch Lomond on the River Leven, watching an artist painting. A man, who I later would get to know as Giovanni Maldini appeared on the bank of the river next to the painter. The next thing I knew, the painter was floating in the river, being swept out into the loch. When I went into work the following day, I found out the painter was the father of my assistant, Anne. After the post-mortem, she told me that he had

had a heart attack and fell into the river, which I can confirm was not true. He was murdered by Giovanni Maldini."

Yvonne paused for a few moments, waiting for the officers to interrupt and question her on why she hadn't reported anything. When they did not, she continued.

"Next was the kid who went into the River Kelvin, Michael. On that night, I was out for a walk and I watched the kids on their bikes for a while. The oldest one, goaded on by his mates, became sexually abusive towards me. Words were exchanged and I walked on, unwilling to tolerate his behaviour when he appeared at the top of the grass embankment. I walked along the path and he shouted, 'hey missus how do you fancy a load of this' as he grabbed his groin. He then came hurtling down the embankment on his bike, so I stopped walking. As he got closer, I took a few steps back and pushed him as he passed me. He lost control of the bike and went into the Kelvin. I thought to myself, *asshole*, and walked on. I heard on the radio the next day he had been found dead in the river. I did not know that he had drowned because he came back up for air and shouted more abuse at me, so while I am sorry he is dead, I did not kill him."

Yvonne picked up her cup of coffee in both hands and took a few sips before placing it back on the table.

"Now, here is the one you know nothing about. Giovanni Maldini was a pervert and was sent here by Leonardo Maldini to seduce me and to keep me away from his son, Lorenzo. I have already told you about what he did at the Leven. He was the ultimate evil, and I was terrified of him. He threatened me and demanded that I meet him on the banks of the Clyde opposite the Science Centre. I remember leaning on the barrier, looking out across the water, just trying to stay calm. The next thing I knew, Giovanni was standing behind me. He grabbed me and he whispered, 'goodbye Yvonne' into my ear. I felt him force me back against the railing and I tried to find a way to defend myself. I will admit I had a locking knife because I did not want to meet him unprepared, knowing what he was capable of, so I pushed it into his stomach. I don't know if he was dead when he went into the water, I just know it was either him or me. At that moment, I chose myself."

As Yvonne looked up with tears in her eyes, reliving her trauma for the benefit of the officers opposite her, she saw them looking at each other in disbelief.

"Are you saying it was self-defence, Mrs Maldini?" inquired DC Russell.

"That is exactly what I am saying."

"Do you need a break?" asked DC Wallace gently.

"No, I am going to wrap everything up in the next five minutes," she replied. She dabbed her crocodile tears delicately from her cheeks, continuing her front of anxious bravado. She wrapped both hands around her coffee cup again, staring into space as if reliving the final act.

"I sold my company to Leonardo Maldini. I did not know that he was a boss in the Mafia. I just love his son and yesterday I married him. Did I beat a Mafia boss? Yes, I did. I took all my clients with me, leaving him with nothing for his one-point-five-million-euro investment. 'Why?' you may ask yourself, well I'll tell you. He treats women, his wife, and his daughter with absolutely no respect. I've seen it, so I decided to teach him a lesson. When he found out what I had done, he was not happy, to say the least. He had lost all that money, simply because he bought my company name and absolutely nothing else. I was completely within my legal right to do what I did. I then bought a controlling interest in his company using his own money. Effectively I have the controlling interest in all his gyms, which is my wedding present to his son."

"Can I ask something?" interrupted DC Wallace

"No, you can't, not yet," she stated. "When I was driving back to my flat after that, I thought I was being followed, so I made a few detours without indicating. I ended up in the car park of The Grove Art Gallery. I got out and I went to the pavilion and waited there, knowing that whoever was following me would not be able to do anything with witnesses about. I was approached by someone I had never met and was told in no uncertain terms that he was here to kill me on behalf of Leonardo. That might sound a bit extreme, but he made no bones about it. I asked him who had sent him, and he said it was Leonardo Maldini. He said he knew everything about me and Giovanni and that I loved sex and that he was the last man I was ever going to have in this life, so he demanded that I start to strip. I knew he was going to rape me. As he got near to me, I lashed out. It was the same as Giovanni, me or him. This is what happens when you deal with gangsters – and I mean real gangsters, not like what we have here in Glasgow. Leonardo Maldini is a mobster."

"Mrs Maldini, let's take a break," said DC Russell, pausing the interview. He pushed himself up from the table and left the interview room abruptly.

DC Wallace broke the silence. "Do you know something? In all my years on the job, I have never heard a story like this. How the hell does a woman like you get into such a mess?"

He caught Yvonne eyeing the tape recorder warily. "It's fine Yvonne, the tape's off," he reassured her.

"What do you mean by a woman like me?"

"Well, you work hard, build up a business, but you fall in love with the wrong guy – or the right guy as he turns out to be, but from the wrong family."

Yvonne nodded knowingly. "Like a book, life has its twists and turns, and nobody knows what is going to happen until the final chapter."

"This is DC Wallace resuming the interview with Mrs Yvonne Maldini. Mrs Maldini, up until now, you have been here voluntarily. From this point on, you are now under arrest."

Over the next ten minutes, her charges were listed, and she was offered the opportunity to comment.

She was charged with the culpable homicide of Michael Bradley.

She made no reply to the charge.

She was charged with the murder of Giovanni Maldini.

She made no reply to the charge.

She was charged with the murder of Riccardo Castanova.

She made no reply to the charge.

Yvonne Maldini was photographed, fingerprinted, and had DNA samples taken before she heard a cell door slamming behind her.

The following day she was remanded in custody pending her appearance at the High Court, Glasgow.

After almost three months in jail, and at the end of a twelve-day trial at Glasgow High Court, the jury picked for the notorious mobster case filed back in, having reached their verdicts on the charges against the accused, Yvonne Maldini.

Yvonne glanced over at her husband and gave him a faint smile, fearing the worst.

The court was packed with members of the public and the press who had become infatuated with a woman from Partick and her links to the Mafia. This was the stuff fiction was made of, yet it had happened in their local community. Two Italian spectators sat in the back row of the court.

"Would the foreperson of the jury please stand," directed the court officer.

A small Glaswegian woman in her seventies, an anonymous member of the public, rose as instructed. Little could she have thought when she received her letter to appear at the High Court Glasgow for jury duty, that she would be standing where she was now.

"Have you decided on the charges on the indictment?"

"Aye, we have," she replied as she handed the court officer a piece of paper, which he in turn handed to the judge who read it and threw it onto his bench.

"In relation to charge one, the culpable homicide of Michael Bradley, what is your verdict?"

"The lassie is not guilty," she answered.

"Is that a unanimous decision?"

"Aye, it is."

"In relation to charge two, the murder of Giovanni Maldini, what is your verdict?"

"Aye, same again, not guilty."

"Is that a unanimous decision?"

"Aye, it is" she repeated.

The murmurs from the public benches started to grow louder, forcing the judge to lift his gavel and strike the sounding block with three resounding thuds.

"Silence please, ladies and gentlemen," he commanded, immediately restoring order.

He turned his attention back to the jury benches.

"In relation to charge three, the murder of Riccardo Castanova, what is your verdict?"

The small forewoman of the jury looked over at Yvonne sitting between the two police officers in the box. She turned and looked at the judge.

"We the jury, having listened to all the evidence, find the accused not guilty," she recited, as if she had just remembered what to say from a television programme.

"Is this verdict unanimous?"

"Aye, it is," declared the woman before sitting down.

Press and media personnel rushed from the court to give their exclusive account of the trial. Each had to be the first to get their coverage out on this golden story.

Yvonne, still in disbelief at the outcome of her trial, managed to raise her head to gaze at Lorenzo. Both of them had tears streaming down their faces, oblivious to the sound of the judge hammering his gavel once more on the sounding block, trying to restore order in the court.

"Ladies and gentlemen of the jury," said His Lordship, "I wish to thank you all for your service over the last twelve days. I watched as you paid attention to all the evidence that was laid before you. I realise that you have had to view some gruesome images and listen to some disturbing evidence and I am recommending that you shall not require to serve on a jury for ten years." He paused and turned his attention back to the Yvonne.

"Would the accused please stand," instructed His Lordship.

The police officers who had been seated on either side of Yvonne throughout the trial helped her to her feet.

"Yvonne Maldini, the jury has unanimously found you not guilty on all the charges on the indictment. You are free to leave the court." He brought the gavel down with one last resounding thud before standing and leaving his court.

Yvonne stepped down from the box where she had sat listening to the evidence against her for the past twelve days. She wrapped her arms around Lorenzo as a free woman for the first time in months.

Yvonne followed the police officers back to the cell area for one last time, and collected her personal property; watch, rings, cash, jewellery, which were returned to her by the court police officer. She was finally free!

"This way please," requested a female court officer as she led Yvonne out of the court building.

"Mr Maldini, I love you so much and we finally have the chance to start a life together. I promised myself that if this moment ever came, I would sell everything. I want to leave here and take you with me."

"Let's go then. We do have a life to start," he agreed as he wrapped his arms around her.

As the foreperson of the jury made her way home from the court, having completed her civic duty, her first thought was to stop off at her local shop and get her husband his favourite meal; fish fingers, chips and beans. By the time she got home, they would be defrosted. *I hope that they have a long and happy life together.*

After all, it was a lovely wedding, she thought to herself, letting a little smile cross her lips.

"This is not over," growled Leonardo to Luca as they made their way from the public benches out onto the streets of Glasgow. "She can run but she cannot hide. If I have to destroy my son also, then so be it."

Gordon looked on as Mr and Mrs Maldini embraced yet again, and was not surprised when she asked. "Are Lorenzo's book, video and YouTube channel up and running Gordon?"

"Of course they are, and for your information, Mrs Maldini, Yvonne Duncan and Company is heading towards one hundred thousand viewers and growing on his channel."

"This is his only viewer today Gordon," she said hugging Lorenzo

"Shall we see you soon Yvonne?"

"Nine o'clock tomorrow, team meeting."

"Gotcha," said Gordon knowing that she was back and in charge.

Epilogue

"*Hola. ¿Hay algo que pueda ofrecerte?***"** greeted the young waitress as she approached the solitary table at the window.

"Hello," replied the woman who occupied it. She had not noticed the waitress approach as she was so absorbed in her work.

"Oh, hello, you are English? My apologies."

"I'm Scottish actually," corrected the woman as she closed the lid of her laptop to give her full attention to the waitress. "It's an easy mistake to make, don't worry." She smiled warmly.

"May I get you something?" asked the waitress.

"Yes, *cortado leche leche* and an iced water please."

"You know about our *cortado leche leche* here on Tenerife?"

"Oh yes, my husband introduced me to it in this very bar, must be about, oh, thirty, thirty-five years ago now. Maybe more," she explained, glancing down at the table as her mind drifted back all those years ago.

A few minutes later, "Señora, your coffee and glass of iced water."

"Thank you so much," she acknowledged, and turned back to open the computer and finish her work for the day.

Later, as the waitress cleared away the empty glasses from the table, she commented that not many English-speaking people came to her home village of Candelaria.

"This place holds so many happy memories for my husband and me. We've visited every year for many years either for a holiday or a short trip. I love this village, which is the reason we bought a house nearby when we retired."

"Oh, what did you do?"

"Back in Scotland I was a nurse and my husband was a police officer." The woman paused before offering out her hand.

"My name is Catherine, and my husband's name is Andrew. We're the Blackmores."

"What you do now? Every time you are in here you always seem so busy, and I never wanted to speak to you in case I was interrupting."

Catherine smiled at the inquisitive young waitress. "I'm an author. And don't worry about coming over to speak to me. Interruptions are sometimes a good thing. I can get so carried away when I'm writing."

"Oh, how exciting!" she exclaimed. "What you are writing about?"

"It's a romance novel set in Glasgow, with some thriller mixed in."

"And what is the name of the book?"

"The Publisher."

"Maybe I get it when it is finished," she commented absently, her tray now full of empty crockery.

"Of course, I can get you a copy. What's your name?"

"Antonia," she said.

"I'm Catherine," she answered extending her hand to Antonia. "What a lovely name. Now, Antonia. There are only two words left on this book, and it's finished." Pausing, she typed them into her manuscript.

THE END.

Antonia peered over Catherine's shoulder to see what she had written. "Is it the end, Catherine?"

"Who knows?" she remarked mysteriously as she packed away her laptop.

"Adiós, Antonia." Catherine rose from the small table and began to wander home under the heat of the Canarian sunshine.

"Adiós, Catherine."

As she meandered up the road, Catherine pondered over what may have happened to Yvonne and Lorenzo after their reunion. *What did his father, Leonardo, and his uncle Luca do to avenge*

the treachery and the killings in the park? One story had been told, but it left
many unanswered questions that had the potential to be their own stories.

"Buenas tardes, Señora," greeted a young, attractive couple as
they walked past hand-in-hand, interrupting her thoughts.

"Buenas tardes," replied Catherine politely, glancing at them as
she caught a hint of Glaswegian under their Spanish. They
walked on down the hill towards the café she had just left.

Catherine exhaled deeply once she closed her front door
behind her. Placing her belongings neatly on the hall table, she
made her way to the sprawling living room that overlooked
Candelaria. She poured a glass of ruby red Italian wine before
sliding open the doors that lead to the swimming pool.

"Who died today?" asked Andy as he lay soaking up the sun.
He lifted his sunglasses and squinted up at her as his eyes
adjusted to the glaring sunlight.

"Could be you if dinner isn't in the oven." She lay down
beside him and kissed his cheek to offset her remark with tender
affection. Not two minutes passed before she sat bolt upright
with a start.

"You okay?" asked Andy, "Something wrong?"

"No, nothing," she replied. Her mind was revisiting the
couple who had passed her on her way home. He was younger
than she, swarthy and fit. She was tall and slim with long red
hair.

The Publisher

About the Author

Born in the northeast of Scotland Simpson moved to Glasgow in the late 1950s spending his formative years in the East-end of Glasgow. His working life was spent in the civil service, forming life-long friendships with those in the Emergency Services. It was those friendships and a love of writing that led him to create this series while he enjoys the quiet life he returned to in the northeast of Scotland.

The Publisher

Other Books by this Author

For The Latest Information On

Available Novels

New Releases

&

Coming Soon

From this Author

Please Visit

JasamiPublishingLtd.com